SARAH VERNON

Painted to Death

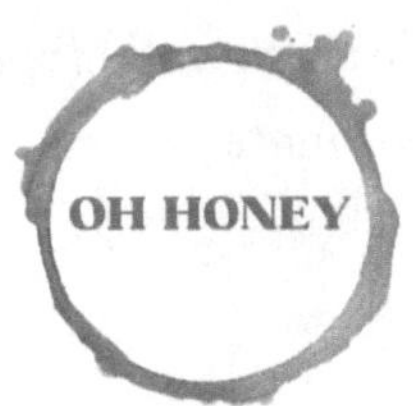

Contents

Chapter One

It was a dark and stormy night. Yeah, for real. That's how I'm starting, because why mess with what works?

Also, it really was dark and stormy the night this all started, the wind bursting in through all the tiny cracks around the old, barely insulated windows of our triple-decker apartment. I say started, but this was actually a couple of weeks after Catherine had died. I just thought I'd start right in the middle of it, because we all know the worst Agatha Christies are the ones where Poirot doesn't even come into it until page seventy-five, and you have to first get through hours and hours of slow English family drama, or worse, a bumbling English inspector.

We were huddled in the living room, with Benny on the floor leaning against the coffee table, and Rebecca, Mel, and me on the couches, mugs of mulled wine steaming in our hands. We would have all preferred to be outside smoking, the distraction of a cigarette easing the conversation, but there's that dark and stormy night again. Plus, our landlord had recently made it harder to disarm the smoke alarm, so no more smoking inside either.

So here we were, trying to have a casual conversation about

a topic that defies casual conversation. Mel – the kind of roommate we weren't quite close to yet, who still attached herself to any kind of group activity at our apartment – was trying hard to make everyone smile, telling unfunny jokes and keeping the wine topped up. Rebecca had taken the comforting aunt approach, keeping her hand on Benny's shoulder while he told us about his afternoon.

"I just feel like they weren't even asking the right questions," he was saying. "It's like, the cops didn't ask about her family much at all – what kind of mood she had been in. All they wanted to know was things like, did she have a boyfriend?" Rebecca tutted and leaned down to pat his back. "I mean, what is this, twenty years ago? Do they still only go for the boyfriend?" Benny frowned into his cup, the steam blurring his glasses.

In fairness, people are still most often killed by their immediate loved ones. And twenty years ago is not all that long ago. But forgive Benny's nearsightedness; in fairness, at twenty-two, it was essentially a lifetime to him.

"What did you tell them?" Mel wanted to know.

Rebecca and I shot her a sharp look, but she was innocently fiddling with her hair, short and newly dyed lavender, and wouldn't meet our eyes. Benny had called us as soon as the police had finished interviewing him, desperate for our company and already on his way over. We had all agreed it would be best not to ask for specifics, but Mel was apparently determined to be as annoying as ever.

"Obviously the truth," Benny replied. "That she had dated a few different people so far this year, but none was particularly serious. And really," he continued indignantly, "even if someone had been a serious boyfriend, how can they actually think that proves anything? All that shows, I think, is how easy it was to love her."

Benny's chin dropped to his chest and Rebecca was immediately on the floor next to him, her arm around his back. I swear she actually said, "There, there."

"Sam, maybe you can get out some extra blankets? Benny, why don't you just spend the night here, on the couch?" Rebecca looked at me expectantly.

"Of course," I said, a clap of thunder accentuating my voice. "It's way too stormy out for you to go anywhere, anyway." I got up, dragging Mel with me. "Mel, help me get the blankets down."

She followed me, obviously reluctantly, out into the hall. I opened the door to the hall closet, still holding onto her arm.

"Sam, what's up? Let go of me," she whined. I rolled my eyes.

"What was all that back there?" I hissed. "We agreed we weren't going to ask him for specifics. Benny's been through enough as it is – we don't have to make him relive everything."

Her eyes grew wide, an expression of innocence we were familiar with, as Mel always proclaimed that she was never the one who left dirty dishes out or forgot to buy toilet paper. It was frankly gross that she would try to pull the same crap here, in the middle of a murder investigation.

"Sorry, I didn't think it was prying just to ask what he answered to one question," she said, still in her most exasperating whine. "And come on, Sam, it's not like you're not curious. Benny was her best friend. Basically her brother! Who else is going to know what's really going on?"

"But you don't need to know what's going on," I said, reaching up to the top shelf for an extra quilt. "If the police want to call you up and tell you everything they've found out in the past two weeks, they'll do that. You don't have to ask Benny for the recap." I pushed the quilt into her arms, turning back for sheets.

"Fine," Mel said. "I'm sorry. But for the record, I've heard you and Rebecca whispering. I know I'm not the only one who wants answers." This last word she delivered in a true crime podcast-perfect whisper.

It was honestly like this with everyone at school – as if Catherine's murder was just one big game, an adventure we were all in on. In reality, the past two weeks had been gut-wrenching. It was only a few weeks after winter break, and we were all just starting to settle in again. Class schedules became routine, and we had even become accustomed to commuting in a particularly snowy Boston February. And then, suddenly, Catherine had died. She was found one morning, collapsed in her studio on campus after a night presumably spent working there. I didn't see her, of course. Poor Benny had found her and had run screaming down to the security guard at the front door. It seemed that, in an instant, the whole building had been turned upside down. Police tape had gone up at the entrance to the senior studios, over Catherine's locker, even at the door to the darkroom, which she managed as a part-time job. Just as quickly, it seemed, everyone in the department had split into one of three possible reactions: giddily morbid curiosity; extreme public displays of mourning by people who had barely known Catherine; and reserved, detached sympathy from those who had actually known Catherine, which unfortunately was the reaction of only a minority of people, mostly just the older faculty who had the sense to be respectful.

I don't mean to make it sound like Catherine didn't have many close friends. She was, in fact, beloved – the kind of person who always had a smile ready, who rarely said a bad word about anyone. Rebecca and I had been friends with her since we'd started college two years before, but it was undeniable that Benny was her closest friend. They had grown up together in the same small town out in Western Massachusetts, coming to school in Boston a year before us and still living together now. I wasn't sure how he was going to get through the rest of the year without her, let alone anything after graduation.

I finished slowly refolding a pillow case and followed Mel back to the living room.

"I'm just grateful, in a way, that her mom isn't here to have to see this. I don't know what that poor woman would have done," Rebecca was saying, doing her sympathetic tutting. Benny's head was still hanging down, a good impression of a marionette who had lost its handlers. "I mean, I know her aunt will be devastated," she went on, "but for a single mother to lose her only child … I honestly can't think of anything worse."

It could've been worse to be Catherine right about now, I didn't say. Sorry, I really don't mean to seem so cavalier about all this. Really. But on some level, you probably know that humor is the best coping mechanism. I just tried not to share these more macabre thoughts with anyone else. Or at least not with Rebecca.

"Come on, Benny," I said instead. "We've got everything ready for you. Let's try to have an early night, and we'll be okay in the morning." I helped him to his feet. "We'll go for breakfast before class, yeah?"

He nodded.

I pulled Mel back off the couch and gestured for Rebecca to follow. Another clap of thunder sounded, closer than ever. We all jumped.

"Let's all just try and get some rest now, okay?"

The next morning was freezing, though for February in Boston, any day with sunshine was a relatively good day. Even after nearly three years, I was barely used to the weather. It seems like there shouldn't be much of a difference between New York and Boston weather, but I definitely could not remember this much snow and ice from my childhood winters. The puddles from the storm the night before had all frozen solid, turning every intersection into a slippery death trap. I kept my head down as I walked, tucking my chin into my jacket to keep the cold out. I needed to get to class early to set up, and had left everyone still sitting over breakfast, quiet and a bit subdued but decidedly better. Benny had even smiled once or twice, after a few cups of coffee.

We lived about a thirty-minute walk from the building our art department was housed in, which meant it was usually faster to walk than risk delays on public transportation. Despite (or perhaps because of) the difficult conversations of the previous night, I was eager to get to class. Although we weren't required to formally select majors that were more specific than the "Fine Art" track we were all on in the art department, I had spent the past two years working mainly with the sculpture faculty. I was no great engineer, but what can I say? I just liked making things. Even when I was a kid, I could spend hours working on crafts, the smaller and more intricately detailed the better. Which is really to say, you know I had a ridiculously extravagant dollhouse in elementary school, every piece of furniture lovingly crafted from whatever I could find in our trash (because even if my parents had been willing to splurge on dollhouse furniture, you could rarely buy the level of detail I was looking for, even if eight-year-old me wasn't quite skilled enough to pull it off). Caps from glue bottles became drinking glasses; the lid from a jar of mustard was filled in with aluminum foil to become a trendy round mirror; pieces cut out from cereal boxes became, well, miniature cereal boxes. I even used photographs of the house in my portfolio when I was applying to school, adding in some conceptual story about investigating the decline of the American middle class and neglecting to mention that it had been a decade since I'd touched any of it. I loved miniatures so much – and this is in the category of macabre thought I would never admit out loud to anyone else – that in the days after Catherine's death, when all of us could see the police coming in and out of her studio and the school buildings, one of my first thoughts was about Frances Glessner Lee. In the early 1900s, this wealthy heiress made twenty miniature dioramas of fictional crime scenes, with ominous titles like "Dark Bathroom," "Red Bedroom," and "Burned Cabin." And it wasn't just an odd hobby. She actually donated these models and helped create the first forensic medicine department at Harvard University. Some police departments even used these models until the 2000s. After the pristine, easy pastime of dollhouse furniture-making in elementary school, I graduated to examining these miniature crime scene models in high school, writing a whole paper about them for a school assignment. Yes, the teacher thought I was bizarre. And yes, the better assignment would have been to recreate one of the models (but I had read that each diorama cost Lee at least three thousand dollars to make, and that was in 1900s money, so no way was I going to fund that). But in any event, in the days after Catherine's death, when we still didn't know many of the details, I couldn't help but picture her studio like one of these forensic miniatures, with art supplies strewn about and bright sunlight pouring down onto this horrible scene through the skylights cut everywhere into the ceilings. I know, it was dark but weirdly comforting to bring everything down in scale. Just don't tell Rebecca.

Even without looking up, I could tell I was getting close to school, because the regular pavement of the sidewalk was replaced with the red-brick cobblestone that demarcated our campus from the city at large. But something was wrong, and I stopped where I was. It was a half-hour before classes started, and ordinarily there would be kids milling around out front, standing and smoking in small groups, no matter how cold it was. Usually, I was one of them. But today, the sidewalk outside the entrance to the art department was empty. I walked slowly up to the door, peering through the glass. Inside, I could see the lobby was filled with students, most sitting at the small tables and couches scattered throughout the space. Instead of the usual lone security guard who sat sentry at the door, there were three guards standing together, apparently still working out the finer points of crowd control. Something was clearly up. I hardly wanted to know what.

I debated for a moment turning around and going home, but the lure of the pottery studio was too strong. That morning's class, "Mineral, Mud, Clay," was one of my favorites, especially since the department had heeded my many pleading notes and finally purchased a series of miniature pottery wheels. That's right, tiny wheels that make tiny vases! And tiny plates, and tiny bottles, and so on. That semester, I was working on a series of tiny Grecian urns, and today several of the forms would be ready to paint, which as everyone knows is the best part. So I pushed open the doors and stepped into the instantly too-hot building.

It seemed like everyone, even the security guards, turned to look at me as I clattered through the doors. As if I were late to an event that no one had announced. I gave some unconvincing apologetic noises and made a beeline for the closest table, winding up next to a senior named Chris. She was sitting back with her long legs stretched out, as if whatever was going on was her new favorite show.

"Hi, Samantha," she whispered, with the kind of smile most people would call crocodilian. She always insisted on calling me Samantha, no matter how many times I told her it was only Sam. "Samantha" was always too Victorian American Girl Doll for me (even though, yes, I know, Samantha is the 1940s doll).

I smiled back and asked, through gritted teeth, what was going on.

"The police are back," Chris said, way too smugly for the circumstances, if you ask me, even adding in a casual toss of her long brown hair.

I refused to flatter her by asking for any more details, instead wanting to know if there was any reason we were required to stay in the lobby.

"No," she said. "We just can't go into the senior studios yet."

Not a problem for me. I fled down the nearest musty staircase to the peace of the pottery classroom in the basement.

Chapter Two

I had just finished setting up the pots of glazes I would need, lining up the bright containers in a neat row on my bench. Peggy, the graduate assistant for our class, was at the back of the classroom, pulling our pieces off the firing racks. She was a pretty clumsy choice for this particular task, and usually dropped at least one piece a week, so I didn't bother to look up when I heard the smash of freshly fired pottery.

Until this sound was quickly followed by someone loudly clearing their throat, too deep and too male to be anyone in the studio – we were a dozen women working in the basement today.

I looked up to see two police officers in the doorway, making apologetic gestures to Peggy, who stood stammering in the back. The younger of the two met my eyes.

"Samantha Green?" he asked. "Would you mind having a quick word with us?" He stepped aside to make room for me to walk out with them.

I looked back longingly at my pots of glazes.

"We're really sorry to interrupt you during class," he was saying now, as they led me down the hall and back towards the staircase. I couldn't imagine where on campus they could be taking me that could possibly be private enough for a police interview, even if it was just a supposedly quick word. Everything, every whispered remark – especially these past few weeks – spread like wildfire in the department.

"It looked like fun back there," he continued.

I guess they were trained to make friends?

"It's okay," I said and smiled. "I'm happy to help. Really. Also, it's Sam. Not Samantha."

"Of course," he replied. "Our apologies. I'm Detective O'Connor and this is Officer Bryson. My supervisor, Sergeant Marks, is upstairs waiting for us." The second officer turned his head at the mention of his name, and nodded down at me from where he towered, six feet over my barely five feet, two inches.

I was silent the rest of our walk. At the top of the stairs, Detective O'Connor led us across the lobby, down a short corridor, and into a small classroom near the back of the building. It was usually used for film classes, with the chairs lined up in neat rows facing a single projection screen. The man waiting inside, presumably Sergeant Marks, had pulled three chairs out of their rows and into a neat little triangle at the front of the room. He smiled and gave me a single nod, gesturing for me to take the seat opposite him, at the tip of the triangle.

"Thanks for coming down here to speak with us," he said. Whatever I had expected a police detective to be, it was almost definitely not this. The man opposite me, who confirmed that he was indeed Sergeant Marks but I could call him Phillip, was tall and thin, reedy enough to be a cartoon grasshopper. His blond hair was thinning yet still stood nearly straight up, almost reaching Conan O'Brien heights. His voice was soft, so much so that even just a few feet away from him, I had to lean over the desk to hear what he was saying. I had seen enough cop shows to wonder if this was some kind of ploy, aimed at knocking suspects off balance.

"We know this is a very difficult time. But I'm sure you can understand that the faster we ask these questions, the faster we can clear everything up and let you go back to your lives," Marks said. "We understand you were a close friend of Catherine Reed's?"

I nodded. I don't know if I would have said close friend, but definitely a good friend. But if they thought I was such a close friend, why had they waited two weeks to interview me?

I must have looked confused, because Detective O'Connor, hereon just "the younger one," broke in.

"We've had a lot of people to talk to over the past couple weeks, as I'm sure you've heard. Your name has come up a few times. It sounds like you were with Catherine earlier on the day we think she died?" At this, he flipped open a skinny black reporter's notebook, something I thought they only did on television.

"Yes," I said. "Catherine, Rebecca, Benny, and I had dinner together at our apartment that Sunday evening. We did most Sundays. I think you already spoke with Benny about this." I raised my eyebrows in question. The pair declined to confirm or deny.

"How did Catherine seem that night?" Marks asked instead, leaning on his elbows in what I took to be his attempt at a casual pose.

"Completely fine," I replied. "She was always a sweetheart, cooking for everyone at those dinners. It was no different that weekend. The next morning, when we got here and heard what had happened … It was just a complete shock."

"Nothing seemed to be bothering her?" Marks went on. "Catherine didn't mention anything that had happened, maybe over the weekend or at school the previous week?"

I shook my head slowly, pretending to consider my answer, but it was going to be the same as for the question before: Nothing out of the ordinary had happened until we heard she had died. *Why were they going on about her mood?* I wanted to ask, but clearly I was not going to be allowed to ask the questions here.

I settled for an answer in a tone that I hoped wouldn't sound too antagonistic: "I really don't think so. Catherine definitely didn't mention anything to me about something stressing her out."

Marks nodded, apparently content. He leaned back, which was clearly O'Connor's signal to take over.

"I'm sorry to tell you this, but we're asking because there may be the possibility that Catherine took her own life."

"No," I blurted out without a second thought. "That cannot be true. Catherine was one of the easiest going people I know." I could hear my voice rising but couldn't stop. "I understand this is something that happens, but absolutely not to Catherine. Catherine was happy." I tried to add a note of finality here, anything that would offset the tremor that had come into my voice.

The two detectives exchanged looks.

O'Connor tried for a conciliatory tone. "Look," he said, soothingly. "We just have to ask and we have to rule out the possibility." Another glance at Marks, who gave the most imperceptible nod I've ever seen. "It looks like Catherine died from a large injection of insulin. Do you know if she often mixed up glucose and insulin? Or miscalculated what doses she would need? We found several empty vials of insulin in her studio, and they do appear to be nearly identical to the glucose she carried."

This was a little bit easier to consider than O'Connor's previous question. Catherine had been diabetic her whole life, and seemed effortlessly at ease with the entire situation. But the fact was, Catherine was forgetful, maybe even flakey; I'd seen her mix up medications and vials once or twice before, although never to this degree. She always caught her mistake before actually taking anything. My pause seemed to indicate this.

"Sam," O'Connor prodded. "Does this sound like something that might have happened?"

I relented and nodded. "Maybe," I said. "But I still have to say, I think that sounds extremely unlikely." I tried to put as much emphasis on "unlikely" as I could muster.

"Okay," O'Connor said, clearly backing off from this line of questioning. "That's okay. We can keep that as a possibility, but we hear that you think it's unlikely. What about anything else you can tell us? Was there anyone you can think of who might have wanted to hurt Catherine?"

Everyone knows this question is coming, don't they? Seems like Police Interview 101 material. You'd think that I would have thought about it, maybe even rehearsed some kind of answer before now. But the truth was, I meant it when I said Catherine was a sweetheart. She never had a bad word to say about anyone, never gossiping with the rest of us – not even when Rebecca got going about whoever's new relationship drama was in the spotlight that week. No matter how much I considered it, I couldn't think of anyone with a good reason to do this. Which is itself an absurd thought: What is ever a good reason to kill someone who's done nothing? I said as much as to the detectives.

"Any recent ex-boyfriends?" Marks cut in. So apparently it wasn't just Benny they were going to ask about this.

"Not really," I said. "She dated Todd – that's Todd Jansen – most of last year, but they broke up over the summer. Maybe mid-August? Before we came back for the new school year. Honestly, he seemed fine with it, and I think he's already dating someone else."

O'Connor nodded, jotting this down quickly.

"Anyone after that?" he asked.

"I don't think she was in any long-term relationships again," I replied, only slightly hedging. "You're probably better off asking Benny about that. If Catherine confided in anyone, it would be him." I paused, hoping that I looked like I was trying to think farther back, when really, I was trying to decide how much information to give them. "I think the only real boyfriend last semester was Michael Drexler." I felt bad giving his name to the police, watching O'Connor add it to his notebook like he was writing up a list of naughty kids for Santa.

Michael was admittedly not my favorite person, but no one really deserved to be added to a police investigation. Todd Jansen would probably be dismissed by the detectives at first glance, with his wire-rim glasses and smooth, easy-going manners, his blond hair and tennis shoes. But Michael: Michael was not the easiest person to get along with, even at the best of times. I didn't know what Catherine had seen in him at the time, maybe besides his looks. He was prickly and arrogant, often needing to be the loudest voice in a class, and made these huge abstract paintings that took up an absurd amount of space in the senior studios. If nothing else, this was just evidence that Catherine was a much better person than I was. I'd never had the patience for Michael that she did.

"What about anyone who might have been jealous of her?" Marks was asking now.

His delivery made it sound like this was a new idea he'd just had, but how could that possibly be true? Wasn't this also Police Interview 101 material – make the interviewee feel like they're getting a behind-the-scenes glimpse? Did these guys think I had never watched a movie before?

"I'm not sure what there really was to be jealous of, exactly. Everyone loved Catherine as far as I knew, but she wasn't exactly the most popular or the richest or honestly the most *anything* that someone could quantify," I said.

"We heard she was up for a big award at the end of this year. When you all graduate?" Marks said.

"Well, not me. I graduate next year; Benny and Catherine are this year," I said. "But yeah, that's true. All graduating seniors are eligible for the Goldstein Award. For artistic excellence."

Marks nodded, considering this. "We've been told Catherine was a front runner."

I shrugged. "I haven't been paying much attention to the award rumors," I said with honesty. "It's determined by a small faculty committee that's supposed to be done in secret, so it's not like we could have had anything to do with it, let alone know who the actual front runners were."

The two seemed content to leave it at this. O'Connor reached behind him, to a folder that was sitting on the next desk over. "Do you think you would be up for answering a few more questions, if we asked you to take a look at some photos?" he asked. "It might be upsetting, but it could be very helpful to us."

It wasn't clear if I really had a choice, or what suspicious something it would imply about me if I refused, so I simply nodded. O'Connor opened the folder, taking out an eight-by-ten photograph and putting it on the desk where I sat.

"Can you tell us if anything is missing or looks out of place?" O'Connor asked, almost apologetically.

I took a deep breath to steel myself before looking down. Mercifully, the photo focused on Catherine's studio, with only her legs visible in the lower right of the frame. At first, all I could see was the beautiful composition, the contrast, the light on the easel in the background making the painting on it even more striking than it was in person, with the painting's three figures shadowy and emerging slowly from the background. Another detail I'd be leaving out when I told Rebecca about this later. I tried to refocus, trying to look carefully at the contents of the studio. In all honesty, most of us worked quite messily, with each of the studios looking like a page out of an I Spy book. It would be hard to tell if anything was missing, let alone out of place. I said as much to the detectives.

"That's okay," Marks said. "Thanks for taking a look. What about in this photo?"

This next one that O'Connor slid over to me focused on her desk. Catherine had painted from photographs, so the desk was a mosaic of photos, negatives, handwritten notes, paint tubes. I slowly shook my head. It was messy, but didn't look *messed with*, exactly.

"I'm so sorry," I said, and I was. "I just can't tell if anything is missing. Everyone's studio looks like this."

"It's okay," the younger one said, smiling sympathetically, "really. We know this isn't easy."

I hoped my smile back was appropriate – concerned and

serious but also acknowledging that I had just noticed he was pretty cute, at least in this lighting, if not exactly my type.

"We'll let you know if we have any other questions, if that sounds okay?" O'Connor said.

Of course I agreed, writing my phone number down and handing it over to him. They stood, gesturing to me that I was free to go. But back in the hallway, I didn't think I could face going back to class and having to answer everyone's questions, even if it meant getting to return to my pots of ceramic glazes. Instead, I walked slowly down the hall, going into the first empty classroom I came to. It was a drawing studio, with chairs lining the edges of two large tables, easels and drawing boards ringing the room.

I sat down, leaning against the easel behind me. Alone now, I couldn't stop picturing the photographs they had just shown me. I didn't know if there really was anything missing, but there was definitely something that had stood out to me. I just couldn't put my finger on what. If Rebecca were here to do her sympathetic tutting, she would say it's the fact that I just saw a photo of a friend of mine dead, and maybe she would be right. But I opened my backpack anyway, taking out a sketchbook and whatever pencils I could fish out of its depths, and started to do what I always did when I was trying to understand something better: I started sketching.

Out of respect, I started with Catherine's body, her legs running parallel along the line that formed the edge of her desk. Over her stood her easel, a rickety metal affair where I had seen her standing and painting nearly every day for years. I added the canvas she must have left unfinished, showing its figures as just a quick line drawing shaded over in short, darker lines. Her paintings recently had been based on black-and-white photographs, mostly family photos or historic, genealogical images.

I didn't know the full story but I knew that Catherine had grown up with just her mom, and the rumor was that she'd never found out who her father was. Then Catherine's mom had passed away from cancer the year before she started school. The whole thing was one of those stories that made the rounds periodically, as details from class critique sessions of her work became gossip. Apparently, her mother had always refused to disclose who her father was, promising that she would eventually, when Catherine was old enough, but of course then she'd died before ever telling her. Catherine had even gotten a copy of her birth certificate after her mom's death, but the line for father had been left blank. Catherine's paintings always kept this kind of shadowy aura about them, the figures (usually her and her mother) all blurry or too dark to make out.

I sketched in the small supply cart she kept next to the easel, filling it with her usual paints and piles of brushes. There hadn't been too many objects on the desk that were clear, but I sketched in whatever I could remember: a notebook, closed; a few random pens and pencils scattered across the surface; a stack of papers, probably reading or an assignment for class; a couple of books with the clear markings of our school library, though I couldn't recall the titles. I put my pencil down, looking at the drawing for any new clues, and groaned inwardly. What did I think I was doing? Clues? It was just a quick pencil drawing of a photograph that might have made a good jigsaw puzzle, but was certainly no masterpiece of detection. I tore the page out of my sketchbook, shoved it into my backpack, and decided to head home for the day.

Chapter Three

The walk home would be good for me. The sun had disappeared behind clouds, but the temperature was a bit better, at least enough that I didn't need to turtle myself quite as deeply into my coat. I still kept my eyes down as I walked, letting the random patterns of gray and black asphalt, the sudden splotches of color from construction spray paint or gum, lull my brain into quieting down, zoning out.

When we first heard that Catherine had died, finding clues was the farthest thing from my mind. In the moment, all that seemed important was supporting one another, making sure Benny was okay, trying not to let the gossip get too out of hand. So what could have just changed my mind in a thirty-minute conversation? Even if it was a conversation with the police, the very idea of "clues" seemed out of place. As the detectives themselves had said, it seemed like Catherine had died from a simple mistake, switching her glucose and insulin. I couldn't remember, but I didn't think they'd even said the word "murder" once in that whole interview.

All the same, would Catherine really have made such a mistake? She had been diabetic for twenty-two years; who would know if she had ever made a similar mistake, going so far as to actually take the wrong medications? I made a mental note to ask Benny, if there was ever an okay moment with him. I didn't even know how much insulin one would have to take to be fatal. How did detectives do it? It seemed like in books, there was always a helpful doctor down the street who would be happy to answer random questions about insulin doses, without suspicion or any hesitation about patient privacy.

I tried to clear my mind again, and let the gray asphalt become the black-and-white tones of the crime scene photographs. I didn't have a photographic memory, but I did pride myself on being able to remember the placement of objects, like the order of paintings in a gallery. It always looked strange in class, but I usually took notes by dividing the page up into different sections, moving clockwise around the sheet. I always remembered things better if I created a map like this.

I tried to move clockwise through my memory of the photographs. The easel at the top of the frame, the painting on it. Catherine on the floor at three o'clock. The desk, with its random but expected assortment of objects. The supply cart next to the easel at eleven o'clock. The placement of everything seemed perfect, not a single item out of place. Not so perfect that it looked staged, but not so messy that it looked tampered with. I sighed, jogging through the flashing lights at the next crosswalk. This was no more helpful than the sketching had been. I didn't even know what I hoped to find.

Looking up, I realized I must have been walking faster than I'd realized. I was just about ten blocks from home, which meant I was only five blocks away from the Phans' store, easily the best convenience store-slash-deli in Boston. I'd first stumbled upon it the day we'd moved into our apartment, which had been a sweltering August afternoon. Rebecca, Mel, and I had moved ourselves, Mel navigating the rented box truck up our twisty, only two-way-in-theory street. By the time we'd finished, I could barely make it back down the three flights of stairs, but needed to venture out in search of dinner. The Phans' shop was the first good-looking place I came to, its windows an eclectic mix of international snack bags and taped-up paper menus. Since then, I stopped in most days on my way home from class.

The bell above the door chimed as I pushed it open, stepping into a blast of overhead heat and the lingering smell of griddled breakfast sandwiches. Stephanie, the Phans' daughter, looked over her shoulder, smiling when she saw it was me. I'd be lying if I said I came here just for the food, which was good and cheap but admittedly pretty standard deli fare. The truth was, whether I'd admit it openly or not, the Phans had become something of a surrogate family for me. I loved my own family, of course, don't get me wrong; they were great, when I got to see them at Christmas and maybe once over the summer. But I had been paying my own way through school from day one, and always had to have at least one job, so I just didn't make it home that much. Stephanie often worked the afternoons, and I'd gotten to know her pretty well over the past two years, especially since we were about the same age as each other. The first time she invited me over for dinner, I'd felt comfortable and comforted in a way I hadn't since school started.

Now, I wandered back over to the counter after picking up a seltzer and a bag of shrimp-flavored chips, idly glancing down each aisle to see if Arun, Stephanie's brother, was stocking shelves somewhere. Unfortunately, he was not. But that was okay, I told myself. I was here to talk murder, not flirt with the person I'd only had a crush on for two years.

I plonked my snacks down on the counter, Stephanie turning around to ring me up. She must have noticed my face, the grimace that had been in place since the detectives had called me out of class.

"Sammy, what's wrong?" she asked, putting the purchases into a small bag. She was the only person who could get away with calling me Sammy. I chalked it up to the fact that she had simply never asked permission.

I sighed dramatically. Steph knew about Catherine and everything that had been going on, and of course she was sympathetic. But I had a feeling that her understanding might not extend to what amounted to meddling in a police investigation. Some people are just funny like that.

"The police came to talk to me today," I started. That was good – a nice, understandable reason to be a bit upset. "They asked me pretty much the same questions they asked Benny."

Steph nodded, having already been texted the full details from last night.

"They seem to think that it might have been an accident, or maybe even that Catherine killed herself on purpose."

Steph's eyebrows knitted together. She did not approve of indecision, apparently even when it came to the police. "Why is there still confusion about it? I would have thought they'd have answers from the lab or the doctor, or whoever it is that examines crime scenes, by now."

I shrugged. "Well, they do know she died from an insulin injection. So, the real question is whether she intentionally gave herself the injection knowing it was too much, or whether she got mixed up and maybe meant to use glucose, so that the whole thing was an accident." I paused, wondering if I should take out the sketches to show Steph. "They even showed me all these photos of her studio, the crime scene." But then I imagined smoothing out a crumpled piece of paper on the counter in front of her, a mess of dashed lines and cross-hatched shadows, and I thought better of it.

"I'm sorry, Sammy," she said. "That must have been really tough to have to look at." She patted me on the hand, turning back to her work at the shelves behind the counter.

I think some people would have found Stephanie a bit harsh, maybe not soft enough, but I loved this about her. I would take her brief hand pat over Rebecca's endless tutting any day.

I let the silence lie for a few moments, while I tried to decide if there was any way to delicately phrase my next question.

"Is it crazy of me to think that I should look into this more?"

"Yes," she said without hesitation, not even bothering to look at me.

Thanks for that, Steph. I slumped harder into the counter.

"I know. But there's something about all this I can't shake, something that just seems wrong."

She turned around from restocking e-cigarette cartridges. "A twenty-two-year-old girl just died, Sam. Of course something seems wrong." She laid a conciliatory hand on my arm. "Also, that's what they all say before diving into some murder investigation they clearly don't belong in."

I wasn't sure who exactly the "they" was meant to be, but clearly it included me and was not a group I should want to be a part of.

"I wish I could show you these photos, though," I said. "There was just something there – or not there – or ..." I trailed off. "I can't explain it. All I know is, Catherine would never have killed herself. Accidentally or not. And I know I saw something that just doesn't make sense."

I was not going to get another hand pat for this dithering. Stephanie turned back to her restocking, and I knelt to cuddle Paul, the calico cat the Phans kept at the store, who had just decided to grace us with his presence, i.e. beg for treats. I leaned over the counter, reaching down to the shelf below it for Paul's bag of treats, putting his allotted three at his feet.

I knew Steph was right. Catherine and I hadn't even been the closest of friends. I'd liked her, of course, and I'd had fun with her. But we were party-on-the-weekend-together friends, sit-next-to-each-other-in-class-if-you-don't-know-anyone-else friends. Not investigate-each-other's-murders-without-question friends. And I'm not some typical detective story protagonist, the "they" Steph presumably meant, who's always filled with alcoholism and inner demons to drive me, despite making zero sense as a motive for actual human behavior. No previous unsolved murder of a family member for me, thanks, and no disappeared sister. Unlike seemingly every other woman my age, I'm not even a true crime junkie (only my mom), because that shit is just too real. But this, this nagging puzzle, whatever it was that I couldn't put my finger on, this was just begging to be solved. Give me an Agatha Christie or Dorothy Sayers any day: nothing pulled me in faster than a classic mystery, a good old who-has-done-this.

I left Stephanie to her work as the lunch-time crowd started to trickle in. Popping my headphones in while I walked, I decided to call my mom as I walked the last few blocks home. I could usually catch her on her lunch break about now.

True to form, she picked up on the second ring.

"Hi honey," she said. "How are you? Everything okay?"

I don't know if this is a script that all moms follow, or just something she had picked up over the years, but this was how my mom started every call, with the double check-in.

"Fine, just fine," I said, giving her a double affirmation in return. "How are you doing? Work okay today?"

My mom, Mrs. Green to her students, was a fifth-grade teacher at the elementary school I had gone to as a kid. It might seem like a cushy job, but between standardized tests and parents, let alone the kids themselves, I knew it could be a stressful nightmare at times.

She exhaled noisily. "Not too bad today. We've got a snowstorm coming tomorrow, so at least there's that to look forward to." The truth was, teachers wished for snow days even more than their students did. "How about there?" she asked. "Are you getting snow tomorrow?"

"No, I don't think so," I said, as she made her usual Mom noises about this being good.

I was silent for a second, long enough for her to correctly read into my pause.

"What's really going on, Sam? Is everything okay there?"

I should have thought this through a bit more before dialing, I realized now. My mom was pretty easy going, but I couldn't see her responding well to the idea that I thought I should start investigating my friend's death.

"I'm okay, really. Just a little shaken up, that's all. The police pulled me out of class this morning to ask me about Catherine." I decided I would start with that and see how it went.

"I'm sorry, honey," she said. "Did they keep you for a long time?"

"No, it wasn't too bad. It's just …" I paused, although I felt bad keeping her waiting, knowing that she'd be on the edge of her seat by now. "Some of their questions made it sound like they're maybe not looking in the right directions."

She seemed to be considering this. "Well, keeping in mind that they might not be sharing all the details with you since it is an ongoing investigation, what makes you think that?"

I could hear snippets from her favorite podcasts between the lines, or in the fact that she actually just used the phrase "ongoing investigation." But her reasoning was helpful.

"They were making it sound like Catherine had killed herself, maybe even accidentally. I just can't believe that would be true."

But no matter how many times I said this, I knew there was more to my investigating urge than just this. I thought I had known Catherine well, but at the end of the day, it was entirely possible that she died by suicide.

"I'm sorry," my mom said again. "I know that must be a hard idea to accept. I think you just have to be patient. I'm sure everything will get cleared up soon."

I left it at that. We made a few more minutes of small talk, moving from the weather to my various aunts and uncles, while I walked up our street and started climbing the stairs to the top floor of our triple-decker. So far, it seemed like I had one solid vote against looking into Catherine's death, and one half-vote that could be for either option, since my mom didn't really know what she was voting for and you could read into her comments either way.

At least, that's what I told myself.

Chapter Four

Since it was still early afternoon, I mercifully had the apartment to myself for a while. Mel worked most evenings after school at a restaurant a few streets over, so she often got home late, but Rebecca could usually be counted on to turn up promptly at half past five.

I grabbed some leftovers from last night's dinner and settled in at the desk in my room. We wouldn't have our own individual studio space at school until next year as seniors, so for now the desk in my bedroom, along with a small bookcase and a few large bins of supplies, was my only permanent workspace. Understandably, it was neither neat nor clean. There were splashes of paint across the surface of the wooden desk and the contents of one of the large plastic supply bins was currently spilling out across the rug in the center of the room, with wooden beads, odds and ends of Styrofoam, and most of an egg carton cushioned in the deep carpet. It would be a nightmare to vacuum, but luckily, I rarely did. On top of the desk was a work in progress, an assignment for the sculpture class I took on Monday and Wednesday mornings. This was the first year I was finally able to take the open studio classes offered in each section, where students could work without specific assignments and be critiqued each week on their self-directed projects. This semester, the sculpture open studio was being taught by Agnes Finel, who was basically my role model for all things art and life. She was probably the oldest professor in the sculpture section, the kind of older woman who's only grown more graceful and regal as the years go by. Agnes (she insisted we call her by her first name, a request made by professors guaranteed to make us swoon) usually wore the kind of simple elegant clothing few people can really pull off – long layers in shades of gray, topped off by a towering mound of silver hair. She was the only person I'd ever known who actually knew how to wear a silk scarf.

Her own work was equally cool, geometric forms in cold smooth granite and marble, objects that looked so perfectly like their materials that you would never guess they were really made of foam and wood and paint, or whatever other materials she could conjure into these new forms. But she was accepting of any kind of sculpture work, unlike other professors who expected their students to be disciples of only their personal style. She even took my work seriously, no matter how miniature, or made of materials that should be or were actually trash.

The piece on my desk I was supposed to bring in and show in class tomorrow morning, but it still wasn't finished. I had recently been revisiting some of the objects from the dollhouse I'd made as a kid, updating them with new materials or designs. This week, I was working on the set of furniture from the original living room: miniature sofa and ottoman, towering bookcases filled to the brim, a few wiry lamps. Only, in this version, I wanted the materials to be clear, for it to be obvious that the legs on the coffee table were really popsicle sticks that still had their brand markings on them, or that the curtains I made (even though there weren't any windows yet, or really even a dollhouse) were actually tissues, hung on rods of cotton Q-tips. Agnes had loved the pieces I'd brought to class so far, and wanted to push me to use more and more disparate materials.

The sofa and ottoman still lay on the desktop, their tufted cushions complete (socks I had cut up and resewn, their athletic ankle bands and gray lines in the toe still identifiable) but missing legs and trim. There were a few different leg options still strewn about, like stacking those wooden beads or breaking apart that egg carton. In any event, there were a solid couple hours of work left. On the other hand, I also had a paper due for my Thursday morning class, a film seminar about media from the Atomic Age. I had written a pretty good outline over the weekend but knew there was a lot more to do before it was due. I hesitated for only a moment before picking up the egg carton.

I only looked up at the sound of the front door, blinking as my eyes readjusted to the dim room outside of the bright spotlight my lamp cast over the desk. I fumbled to find my phone in my pocket. It was already after five o'clock. I heard Rebecca calling down the hall, and got up to greet her, gingerly propping up the nearly finished sculpture against a small tube of paint.

Rebecca seemed surprised to see me. She had just put her backpack down and was unpacking a few bags of groceries on top of the kitchen table.

"How long have you been home?" she asked. "You don't usually beat me here."

I picked up a container of coffee and turned to put it in the cabinet. I had been so focused on working all afternoon, I hadn't had time to decide how much I wanted to tell Rebecca about this morning. I didn't think I could do a repeat of the previous evening, and in all honesty, she deserved a break from always being the supportive one.

"Why don't I cook dinner tonight?" I said instead of answering. "I'd be happy to. We got out of class early this afternoon, so I had some extra time."

Rebecca looked at me warily. I was a perfectly generous roommate, but it's true I didn't usually offer to cook. Nor was my cooking really that good.

"That sounds nice," she said slowly. "I'll open a bottle of wine. We can cook together."

I grinned, forever impressed at her diplomacy, and once again thinking what a great mom she would be.

"Toss me that package of pasta," I said. "I'll get it started."

We worked in silence for a few minutes, Rebecca chopping onions and garlic for a sauce while I got a can of crushed tomatoes simmering. Once everything was bubbling away nicely, we both sat down at the small kitchen table, leaning back in our mismatched chairs. She had poured a small glass of wine for each of us, and was now idly swirling hers.

"How about you?" I asked. "How was your day?"

Rebecca had always been one of the more serious in our group of friends, but recently a small furrow had shown up between her eyebrows, a line of concern I rarely saw her without since Catherine's death. I wouldn't be surprised if I soon saw a few gray strands appear in her blond hair.

She sighed, then seemed to collect herself. "Not bad, usual Monday." She smiled thinly, pausing. "I had lunch with Benny today."

I nodded, but didn't ask anything further. With Rebecca, sometimes the best thing to do was to sit and wait, let her tell you whatever she wanted to in her own time. I could see her jaw clenching and unclenching, as if she was literally chewing over her next words.

"Sam, I'm really worried about him," she said finally. "You know how I mentioned the other day about wanting to find him some help? Someone to talk to right now? A professional, not just us." I nodded, noting how generous it was of her to say "us" and not "me," since she had taken on most of the emotional work these past few weeks. "Well, I tried to bring this up with Benny over lunch. But he's just so resistant to the idea. He kept saying he would be fine, he just needed to work through it on his own." Rebecca paused again. "I'm worried I pushed a bit too far, because eventually he snapped at me, something about how I might believe in therapy but that's not the way everyone was brought up. As if I should be ashamed for even thinking that he would need help right now."

I felt my anger rising. I was always quick to jump to people's defense, but especially Rebecca, and especially in this situation. Who could possibly say she had done the wrong thing by suggesting a counselor? But I knew that wasn't the response Rebecca was looking for here. I stayed quiet, instead standing up to stir the sauce.

I could understand where Benny was coming from. He'd been raised in the kind of staunch, pull yourself up by your bootstraps New England family that stayed true to their Puritan roots, even all these generations later. Compared to my mom, who usually shared a bit too much about her coworkers' love lives or students' family issues, Benny's parents hardly ever said a personal word. I had only met his father once, when he'd come up for an exhibition at the end of my first year, but the man had made a lasting first impression. He was not exactly a formidable figure, but a trim man who stood shoulder to shoulder with Benny's five seven or five eight. I was never clear on what he did, exactly, only that he'd worked at a financial management firm for decades, building it up into a veritable empire of telling other people what to do with their money. For all his senior year bluster about day jobs and gallery representation, this was the real reason Benny never seemed truly worried about what he would do after graduation. When Mr. Stockton had died suddenly of a heart attack last year, we'd all assumed that Benny's future was set. I know this seems like a crass thought to have at the time, and obviously we never asked Benny about it directly. But the rest of us were barely employable as gallery receptionists and had a long future of minimum wage ahead of us, so it was fair that this would be on our minds.

I turned back to Rebecca, who still sat staring into her glass. "I think you just have to let it go for now. Let Benny come to the idea on his own, you know. Let him think it was his idea in the first place." I smiled encouragingly.

Rebecca nodded slowly. "Yeah, I know you're right. It's just a very hard situation to watch."

I patted her on the back as I slid past her chair, getting the colander out of the pantry to drain the pasta.

Once we were both sitting back down, glasses refilled and spaghetti served, I decided to make my own suggestion.

"Maybe it would be good for you to speak to someone," I tried. "You've been doing so much for everyone else, I think it could be good for you to have more support for yourself."

She made some noncommittal noises, but I knew Rebecca

well enough to know this wasn't an outright dismissal. She thought about everything carefully, thoughtfully, not just her words. Knowing her, we would drop this topic now, only for her to bring it up again in a few days after she'd taken her time to think it over. So I didn't push any further in the moment, instead pretending to be absorbed in the food.

Rebecca put her fork down and was looking at me curiously now. "Sam, why did you really leave early today? We looked for you at lunch to join us, but we couldn't find you."

I paused mid-bite, wondering how slowly I could chew to buy myself time without looking like an actual farm animal. Of course I couldn't lie to Rebecca.

"The police came to talk to me this morning. I left after that." I looked up. Rebecca's eyebrows had knitted back together, the furrow as deep as ever. "It's okay, really. I just didn't feel like talking much or being around everyone after that." I tried my most convincing voice: "It was completely fine, but you know what the department is like when you don't feel like being social. Class was just too much to go back to."

Rebecca nodded and I hoped she would leave it at that, but of course I should have known better. I wound up giving her the same rundown I had told Stephanie earlier, but again leaving out my post-interview crime scene sketch or my memory palace walkthrough of Catherine's studio.

When I finished talking through the detectives' questions, the information they had shared (or let slip, though Marks clearly had the imperceptible signaling down pat), Rebecca had finished eating.

"No," she said simply. No anger, no defiance. Just a simple statement of what we both knew to be true.

Despite what the detectives had suggested, Catherine

couldn't have killed herself. Although I had been ruminating on this all day, hearing someone else confirm my thinking seemed definitive. Our eyes met as we silently acknowledged what this must mean.

"So, you do realize," I started slowly, not sure how directly I should or could make this next statement, and finished in a rush before I could change my mind. "This means we think someone else killed Catherine."

Rebecca was still sitting, poised, with a calm and determined expression. She nodded simply.

"I know that sounds extreme, but I think that has to be true. We both know she was happy; she had no reason to kill herself. She would have talked to us if there was something going on," Rebecca reasoned. "And I know you said you'd seen her get the medications mixed up before, but I think this would have taken a lot of insulin. Catherine would have realized and stopped. Also, I remember she wasn't drinking that night, since she knew she wanted to go back and work in the studios. She wouldn't have been especially clumsy."

I let these statements sink in. Even if we agreed that Catherine's death had been murder, did I really think Rebecca would be any more encouraging of my investigating than Stephanie had been? She might not always be as outspoken as Steph, but Rebecca would never think twice about warning you away from a bad idea. If I wanted someone on my side in this, I would have to work hard to convince her it was a good idea.

"The thing is, I don't think the police will necessarily agree with us. I did try to tell them how impossible I thought their scenario sounded," I said. "And they dropped it, eventually, but I don't think they're going to take my word for it and leave at that." I paused, hoping Rebecca would get to the next logical point without making me say it.

"Maybe we should ask Benny to call them – he could go back and talk to the detectives about this again," Rebecca said.

"Sure, we could do that. Or, maybe I could look into it a bit more first."

Rebecca's eyes hardened, taking on the look they get right before she tells me off for leaving dirty laundry lying around or having too many lights on.

I rushed on, trying to cut her off at the path. "That way, we could go to the police with more information, a bit more background on why we think it couldn't have happened the way they said." Her face softened somewhat.

If I do say so myself, I think this sounded as good a reason as any to jump into a murder investigation.

"Even if you do look into what happened," Rebecca said slowly, emphasis on if, "where would you even start? I can't think of anyone who would have any reason to hurt Catherine. She was one of the nicest people I know."

I know what a cliché that can sound like, but Rebecca definitely had a point. It would be hard to think of anyone who would have a motive for doing this. It wasn't just that Catherine was nice, but she was quiet, easy to get along with. She was almost easy to overlook, until a few weeks had gone by and you realized she was the only person in class who had actually done all the work, never been late, and always had something constructive to say about everyone else's work. Catherine was quietly determined, a work ethic I usually put down to her upbringing with a single mom. I knew it couldn't have been easy, and like me, Catherine was only here because of financial aid and her part-time job. As supportive as Rebecca could be,

Catherine was the one you would want to go to with any kind of practical problem, like dealing with a professor or completing a project. She could always be depended on for solutions.

But maybe we were approaching this the wrong way. Death wasn't fair, and people died all the time who hadn't done anything wrong. It seemed like we couldn't start by only looking for a "good" reason why someone would want to do this. I said as much to Rebecca.

"That's true," she said, considering. "I guess it could have been a stranger? Some disturbed person who happened to wander into the building? You know the security there isn't exactly strict." She said this last part almost brightly, and I could understand why. The possibility of a stranger meant that it couldn't be anyone of us, anyone Catherine knew. I would have to tread lightly on this topic with Rebecca.

"That's certainly a good point," I said. "I'm sure the police will be looking into that idea. In the meantime, let's just give it some more thought, okay? I know it sounds far-fetched, but I'm sure there's something we can do or find that'll be good to bring back to the detectives."

Rebecca nodded, doing the jaw clenching again as she considered her next words.

I stayed silent until finally she decided to speak: "What about Thompson?"

Our eyes met. Thompson meant Professor James Thompson, longtime painting professor. His portraits were known for being something out of a movie, with huge figures set against theatrical backdrops in stark lighting and deep shadows. The man was hardly less dramatic than his paintings, always involved in whatever the latest uproar was on campus, from fair pay for graduate assistants to switching to paper straws in the cafe. But simply being dramatic didn't mean he was capable of murder. And I knew this wasn't what Rebecca was thinking. Because you know how there's always that one professor whom all the female students know about, even if they've never taken a class with him? And not because he's cute. Thompson was that professor, whispered about in the women's bathroom and in glances, in unspoken exchanges in class. Catherine had been in his open studio section all year, preparing a set of paintings for the graduating students' exhibition. We all knew that she had been spending every spare minute in the studio, meeting with him during his office hours for additional critique.

"As far as I know, Catherine hadn't been having any problems with him," I said.

Between the lines, we both knew what this really meant: neither of us had heard any rumors about the two of them, anything to suggest she was the latest student he had approached.

"Catherine might not have said anything to us," Rebecca countered. "I know it sounds extreme, but I think if we're trying to come up with alternate explanations, he should at least be considered."

I had never taken a class with the man but had heard enough about his behavior to see the sense in this.

We agreed to leave it at. I almost told her not to tell anyone else about this conversation, then thought better of it, not wanting to spook Rebecca any more than I already had. I didn't want her to think that I already considered everyone in our circle, in our department, to be a possible suspect. If I had learned nothing else from years of overhearing my mom's true crime podcasts, it was that a person is much more likely to be killed by someone they know than a total stranger.

"Well, in any event, did you manage to get time off for next

Wednesday?" Rebecca asked, forcing a subject change.

"Oh, yes. Thanks for the reminder. I was able to switch shifts, so I can make it all day."

Seemingly minutes after her death, the school had announced that they would be holding a memorial exhibition for Catherine, a show of her paintings. Benny, Rebecca, and I had agreed to arrange it, and would spend next Wednesday hanging a group of eighteen paintings in the school gallery. I wasn't exactly looking forward to this task. I'll be honest: like many artists, installing work is my least favorite part of making something.

I helped Rebecca clear away the dishes, then made a (true) excuse about needing to finish an essay, and went back to my room, settling into bed with my phone and laptop. I texted Stephanie first: *R votes for investigating, you've been overruled.* She immediately replied with a thumbs-down emoji and a few choice words about my common sense that I won't repeat.

I opened the laptop, clicking open my essay outline so that I could at least tell myself that I was actually working on homework. But I also wanted to start thinking about Catherine's death and the people around her, before Rebecca thought better of it and came in to tell me off. I looked up Catherine's social media accounts, but already each page was buried in memorial posts about how missed she would be. It would take me ages to scroll back through these to get to her actual posts. Instead, I settled for checking the photos she'd been tagged in most recently. The album was the usual mix of student events, a gallery reception the month before, a few shots of her and Benny over winter break. They were from the same town in Western Massachusetts, so usually drove back together for the holidays. Catherine's aunt had come to live with them during her mom's last months and had stayed after her death, so Catherine still went back there for breaks.

I don't know what I was looking for exactly, but there certainly weren't any photos of someone hovering over Catherine with a murderous look in their eye. I opened up my email instead, scrolling through for the last group thread we had. Rebecca, Benny, Catherine and I had been planning a trip together for the summer after Catherine and Benny graduated, a few days in California (chosen solely because we were planning while it was the middle of winter in Boston). We had sent a few notes back and forth over winter break, Rebecca sending details of various vacation rentals and the rest of us responding with thumbs up and funny GIFs. Catherine had sent a photo of her and Benny in party hats and fake mustaches, going through boxes of childhood things in Benny's attic.

I think this was as much as I was going to find of Catherine online: someone who loved her friends, who worked hard at school and kept her head down. If I was really going to find out anything new about her, or at the very least more personal than this, I would need to look in the one place she seemed most herself: her studio.

Chapter Five

So I decided to just lightly poke around, definitely nothing that would involve capital "I" Investigating. Just a light rummage in Catherine's studio before class. Snooping, if that wasn't such a dirty word. The police tape had come down, so technically it was open to anyone now, even if the police were still at school and still interviewing (or just having "quick chats," or whatever they wanted to call it). Especially to anyone with a valid reason for being there, like that I'd lent Catherine a pencil the week before she died and I definitely needed it back now. Not a weak excuse at all, thanks.

When I walked into school that morning, through the groups of smokers back in their rightful places, the lobby was silent compared to the previous morning, emptied of gawkers. Still, there was a slight fizz in the air, an electric current running through the hallways that I very much hoped was not just me. I had nothing to be nervous about, I reminded myself while I made my way upstairs, trying to remember how I usually walked – casually. I was just looking for a pencil.

The senior studios were on the top floor of the building, the better for taking advantage of the skylights cut throughout the roof in regular intervals. Catherine's studio was in a large room on the east side of the building, with one whole wall of windows to catch the morning light (and the lights from the jumbotrons during Red Sox games in the evenings). Each studio suite had room for eight to ten students, partitioned out evenly with temporary, movable walls on wheels, walls pockmarked with the push pins, occasional graffiti, and intentional and unintentional paint smears of a thousand previous students. The studios would empty out at the end of each year, to be reset and refilled in the fall. Some people would leave their small white cubicles nearly empty, choosing to hang up only one piece at a time while they worked on it in a minimalist heaven, while others did their best to turn their studio into a living room or bedroom, with heaps of cushions and fabric hung up on the walls. Inevitably, squabbles would break out between the two factions, with the former accusing the latter of unnecessary noise and mess. The faculty tried not to get involved, only shuffling students around if they absolutely had to. I'm sure they were thankful for the rotating schedule that meant each professor only served as a senior mentor for one semester at a time.

Catherine had been the former bare walls type, while her studio neighbor, a girl named Julia, who made paintings of animals and snack foods, was the latter. Julia's cushions and blankets spilled out of her cubicle, and you could still see where Catherine had tried to gently tuck the fabrics back under the temporary wall between them. It was one of the larger suites of studios, so there were nine other students who worked in the room: Benny; six other girls whom I knew to smile at but never spoke to beyond a hello; and three senior guys, the less said about them the better. They were the type we could all easily picture in ten years' time: putting giant, probably rusty, steel sculptures of basic geometric shapes up at the kind of huge, empty warehouse space favored by contemporary modernist galleries and commercial art fairs. In other words, the three of them were basically interchangeable white men in different colors of baseball caps, all working through the same macho crap. On the plus side, there's still a lot of money in large rusty sculptures.

Stepping into Catherine's studio now, still washed in nine am sunlight only slightly weakened for it being winter, I was overwhelmed by a feeling of familiarity and nostalgia. The space still smelled like oil paint and turpentine, chemical but comforting, laced with the faint hint of stale coffee and old paper, as if Catherine had just stepped out to lunch and would be back and picking up a paintbrush at any moment. The only place in the building that smelled better to me than any of the painting studios was the darkroom, where I had worked in a work study position my first year here. Nothing was as Proustian for me as the smell of photo developer (especially since I had once spilled about a gallon of it all over myself), but oil paint and coffee came pretty close.

Although I knew that the police had been through everything, presumably dusting for fingerprints and whatever else they could find, it still felt like Catherine had been the last person to touch these things, to use the pens scattered across the desk or flip through these books. I was almost afraid to touch anything, as if I would wipe off any remaining trace of her. I gingerly reached out and picked up a pencil, using the end of it to tip open the book sitting on top of a small stack: *Fathers on Film: Paternity and Masculinity in 1990s Hollywood*. I couldn't remember Catherine mentioning a film class this semester, but the topic was certainly fitting for her.

I sighed and sank down onto the desk chair. If I was really going to do this, I would have to really do it. No more gingerly poking around, no more sitting and looking. Before I could think twice, I picked up the whole stack of books and pulled them into my lap, flipping through each one before re-placing it on the desk. There was one more film book about women directors and violence, a book of Eric Fischl paintings (gestural, colorful figures against idyllic Hamptons backgrounds), and one book I wasn't quite sure what to make of: *The Claims Process: Administrative and Judicial Methods*. From the table of contents, it looked to follow the paternity theme of the first book, as far as I could tell. I made a mental note to try to find Catherine's class schedule for the semester. We weren't quite as sequestered over here in the art department as it sometimes seemed, so it was entirely possible that Catherine had been taking classes in sociology or gender studies, even an elective in the law school.

There didn't seem to be anything else of particular interest on the desk, and unfortunately it was more of a long metal table than a desk, so no deep or hidden drawers to go through here. I took a few photos of the desk just to be safe, turning to get a picture of the easel and the rest of the space as well, even taking one of Julia's fabrics spilling under the wall. Judging by the lack of a sketchbook or pages of notes lying around, I assumed the police had taken away anything I might have also been interested in. Inconsiderate of them, but reasonable, I thought. I couldn't see Catherine's bag anywhere, either, so assumed this was probably with the police, too. Just as well, since if she was anything like me, it would be an entire backpack filled only with fifteen pencils and two tampons.

I swiveled around in the chair, rolling the couple feet over to the easel and supply cart. I made quick work of the cart, going through the three or four dozen tubes of paint, assorted paint brushes, tin of turpentine, and pad of palette paper pretty quickly. With a judgy artist's eye, I couldn't help but notice the store brand she usually worked with, and the synthetic colors she seemed fine with. What can I say, my first painting teacher was a hardcore stickler for historical methods, limiting our palettes only to colors that would have been available five hundred years ago. Yeah, okay. I can be as much of a snobby jerk about art as the next artist.

As I had seen in the photos the police had shown me, Catherine's most recent painting was still sitting propped up on her easel. It was a standard school-issued easel, covered in decades of peeling paint and tape and forever wobbly, never quite level. Catherine had done her best, adding a stack of thin magazines beneath the right front leg. The painting was large by Catherine's standards, about thirty-six by forty inches, and an image that at first glance looked like a washed-out black-and-white photo, all grays and blacks. But the closer you looked, the more other colors emerged: shades of blue and ochre turning the grays darker in some places, forming highlights in others, bathing the scene in the kind of tinged lighting of a very old photograph that's been left out in the sun. The three figures in the scene were arranged in a line, as if they were actors working out their blocking from stage left to stage right. In the foreground, a figure stood awkwardly turned to their left, wedged into the corner of the canvas. Directly behind them, only half visible, was a figure who looked like a slightly larger version of the first. Both seemed to be female, but were so washed out in gray light, it was hard to discern what, exactly, their distinguishing features were. Behind and to the left of them was a third figure, the one with the most of their body in the frame. If they were actors, this would be the one to get the spotlight's attention. The same gray washes covered this figure as well, but it was almost like mist here, opening up from the fog enveloping the front two figures. I wasn't sure why, but I thought this figure was probably male. It might have been the simplicity, the straightforward stance of a person who seemed to be standing with his hands in his pockets, turned towards the front two figures. But, of course, this is the problem with art: I could have said that the painting was of three lions or three knights in shining armor or three ice-cream cones, and it would be pretty much just as believable. It's not that Catherine's paintings were abstract, just quietly impenetrable. More or less like their painter, I guess.

I was startled out of these not-so-deep musings by the sound of a heavy object being plunked down, a chair scraping across the floor. At first I thought Julia had somehow snuck in past me, but when I poked my head out of the cubicle, I saw a desk lamp had been turned on in Benny's studio. He was still standing in the entrance between his temporary walls, backpack in hand on the floor, desk chair pulled out. He turned at the sound as I got up to greet him. For a split second, I was terrified I would have to explain what I was doing in our dead friend's studio before class, but mercifully this was not his first question.

"Morning, honey," he said, coming over to me and giving me a peck on the cheek.

We stood silently for a moment, looking together over Catherine's space. Benny sighed.

"I've been coming in here, too," he said. "Just to sit, be with her."

He put his arm around my shoulder. Yes, this was good; I

could use this. Just a grieving friend here, folks, nothing to see. No snooping at all, really. I smiled sadly, an expression I really should have practiced given how oxymoronic that sounds, but didn't say anything. Without shrugging off his arm, I just started to shuffle us out of Catherine's space and diagonally across the room, staying silent while I led us to his studio.

Benny gave my shoulder one last squeeze and moved past me into his studio, tapping the back of the chair to indicate I should sit. He hefted his bag up onto the table, unzipping it to reveal a colorful stack of papers.

"I was up all night," he said, with the zeal of someone whose enthusiasm would probably run into their exhaustion in precisely one hour. With Benny, you never quite knew which would win out. I had always known him to pull all-nighters in the studios, working till all hours when the idea for a new painting came to him, pausing only for a disco nap on the couch in the library as needed. Like Catherine, he had been dealing with family history in his paintings lately, though in a far more Kodachrome style than Catherine's grays. Benny worked on large canvases overlaid with a snapshot-size grid, rows of five-by-seven or four-by-six rectangles filled in with images out of someone's family vacation slideshow. Not mine, of course – we were always too poor for the cruise ships and ski passes of Benny's childhood – but at least I could be thankful that my dad never looked as angry as his did in every single one of the images.

"Rebecca called me after you guys talked last night," Benny was saying.

Of course she did. I kicked myself for not saying something to her about keeping it to ourselves. Benny wasn't suspect number one, but it would probably be better if there were fewer people involved in this. Nancy Drew only had two friends, right?

"You know, the police never talked to me about their little theory that Catherine died by suicide." The way he said "little theory" made it clear what he thought about this idea.

I nodded in sympathy, waiting to see where this was going.

"I know I don't have to tell you what a ridiculous idea that is, but it did get me thinking."

I loved Benny, but had learned early on it was best to wait during these sparks of inspiration, lest I inadvertently agreed to participate in a drag fashion show again.

"Even if the police are completely wrong about this, it could be a beautiful way for us to honor Catherine …" Benny drew out one of the papers from his bag with a flourish, handing me a neon-pink flyer that read "Student Mental Health Support" in bold all caps at the top. There was a date and time below this, and a quick line drawing of an old school rotary phone with a handwritten note that read: "Dean Winters, it's time for a conversation."

I puffed my cheeks out and exhaled noisily. I was pretty sure I knew where this was going and didn't especially want to be involved in anything that could antagonize the administration, but figured I'd wait for Benny to spell it out for me first.

"Yeah, Benny, this looks great. I think this could be an important idea," I said, nodding up at him. "What, uh … What's the conversation you want to have, exactly?"

He beamed. "Well obviously, if there's even talk of the possibility that Catherine could have killed herself, then the school needs to be doing more for us. It's not just about some clinic in the basement; it should really be a community-wide effort."

I struggled to contain my face, going for a sage nod as best I could. Again, all my love to Benny, but sometimes he forged ahead with ideas like this with a complete disregard for the existing facts. That little clinic in the basement? It was actually a set of about six highly skilled social workers and therapists, whom I saw working late here even more often than I saw Benny working late.

"Well, I think this is really important, Ben. Let me know if I can do anything to help," I said.

I know, I know. I might complain about it, but at the end of the day, I almost never said no to helping Benny. The drag fashion show wound up being a ton of fun, after all, and I still have the long blond wig to show for it.

"Thanks, Sam," he said, grabbing another handful of the flyers from his bag. "Could you hang these up today, please? I want as many people at this first event as possible. I'm hoping we can come up with a list of needs that I can take to the dean."

"Sure, no problem," I said, taking the flyers and stifling a sigh. Hanging up flyers was one thing; confronting Dean Winters something entirely separate and definitely worse. It's not that he was intimidating, exactly, and in fact made every effort to make students feel welcome and like we could approach him. But at the end of the day, I was here only because of my scholarship and my work study job, and it didn't seem like a bad idea to fly below the administration's radar.

"I'll get these up today," I assured him, tucking the flyers under my arm.

I stood to go, bumping into a painting that leaned against the wall as I turned. "Shoot, I'm so sorry, honey," I said, propping the painting back up. It was half finished, with two rows of images filled in. The painting was full of intense sunlight, as if each image had been painted from a blown out, over-exposed photo. "This one is really nice, Benny," I said, taking a step back to admire it.

"Thanks. I don't think I can finish it, though," he said. "I was working on it last month, before Catherine …" Benny trailed off.

"Yeah, that makes sense," I said gently, giving his arm a soft pat. My hand had come away wet from the painting, so the pat was more of an awkward attempt with the back of my hand, as I tried not to rub oil into his sweater. "Well, as I said, I'll get these flyers up today, and maybe I'll see you for lunch?"

We said our goodbyes, and I tried to act casually as I went back to Catherine's studio to grab my bag. With one last air kiss to Benny, I left the room with just enough time to get to class.

Down on the second floor, Agnes had already gotten us ensconced in one of the sculpture classrooms. This open studio section was about fifteen of us, mostly women. I was one of only two juniors in the class, along with a girl named Mary, a sweetheart who made kinetic, Rube Goldberg-esque creations. I put my things down on the table next to her, careful not to bump any of the supplies she was already laying out: a roll of aluminum foil; a box of four-inch-long screws; a set of sieves. You know, the usual things you might need by ten am on a Wednesday morning.

When about ten of us had gotten settled, Agnes looked up from her seat at the front of the room and beckoned us over, making pleasant small talk about the weather as we dragged chairs closer to her. Since we met twice a week, we used one class as a critique session, and the second to work independently. This, like any other class policies, had been decided together with Agnes, who had the ability to make students feel like they were the ones making choices she had already decided, an ability that could only come from a thirty-year teaching career. Today was a critique day, and most of us had already unpacked our sculptures, setting up around the room. My little sofa and ottoman stood alone on a work table, unadorned but, I thought, holding their own in a room full of louder, bigger work.

Agnes had us turn our attention to the first work, a blobby form with multiple components attached together. The only discernible material was bubble-wrap, which seemed to hold a plethora of other, unidentifiable objects. The girl who'd made it was a senior with long black hair, streaked with pink and royal blue highlights – hair she was playing with now while she explained to us her thought process, her methods. I gave her my full attention while I slowly slid my phone out of my pocket, tapping it on without looking down. With only the briefest of glances, I managed to send Stephanie one of the photos I had taken in Catherine's studio that morning, the one that showed most of her desk, with the easel in the background. I added a quick caption: *Nancy Drew meet-up this pm?* Her reply came quickly, though she ignored the photo. I could see I would still need to work on her acceptance of all this, but at least I could do so that night over dinner at her house.

The bubble-wrap sculptor was still talking, though even Agnes showed signs of waning attention. She was nodding along as the girl talked about translucency and form, but even from across the room you could tell the smile didn't make it up to her eyes. Not for the first time, I wondered how Agnes put up with decades of students who prattled on obnoxiously about their capital "W" Work (and also not for the first time,

I sincerely hoped she didn't include me on that list. I always tried to keep my critique preamble to a tight thirty seconds, max).

Eventually, we made our way around the room en masse, breaking for five minutes at a time between viewings of various abstract assemblages, shiny black orbs, and gilt-encrusted organic forms. I'll spare you the gory details of what was said about my work, but overall, it's been positive. It's always a bit excruciating to be the focus of a critique in class, and I really should have been nicer about the first girl. It's easy to seem like you're speaking in sound bites when you're standing in front of a group of your peers, some definitely judgier than others, trying to explain why and how you made something, something you're now asking them to look at and consider seriously. I never enjoyed being the center of the attention, and as grateful as I was for positive, constructive criticism, I was always equally grateful when my turn was over.

At twelve-thirty, we slowly started to pack our things away, the other girls heading out in groups of two or three. Agnes was just putting her notes away and stood to leave when I caught her eye.

"Are you heading to lunch?" I asked, my voice always sounding a bit shy and halting around her.

She smiled warmly. "Samantha! Join me."

Okay, so Steph wasn't the only person who got away with calling me Samantha. Obviously Agnes could call me whatever she wanted.

We walked down to the cafe on the first floor together. I was always aware of how young I was when I was with her, how much I slowed down to accommodate her pace, even though she was a trim, fit woman, and the reality was she could probably run circles around me, especially after a day in the studio spent hefting heavy materials into place.

Settling down to a table with our coffees and sandwiches, Agnes started asking me about my plans for next year. "Have you thought about whom you want to work with for your senior year? Professor Phallen, maybe?" she asked, mentioning another sculpture professor.

We would each choose two advisors for our senior years, who would serve as mentors while we got ready for the graduating student exhibition. I took a bite of my sandwich to stall for time, gingerly wiping away a smear of avocado before answering.

"I was actually thinking I might talk to Professor Thompson about next year," I said, not quite able to meet her eyes.

Agnes paused mid-sip, then seemed to quickly recover.

"Are you thinking about doing more painting? Thompson is certainly competent, but I might not have thought of him as a first choice for someone with a sculpture focus."

She gazed at me thoughtfully while I tried to find a good explanation, something more plausible than, *I'm looking for an excuse to talk to him about my friend who was probably murdered, maybe even by him.*

"Well, I know Catherine had spoken highly of him, and she seemed to really enjoy working with him. I thought maybe a fresh perspective would be a good thing," I said.

Agnes nodded, though still with the thoughtful look on her face.

"And how are you doing? After what's happened with Catherine? I know you two were close," she said, reaching her hand across the table for me to take.

"I'm okay," I said slowly. "It's obviously a lot to process, and everyone is terribly upset – Rebecca and Benny especially, of course." I paused. I had of course been truthful so far, and I felt bad needing to ask Agnes such a leading question next. But just as in Catherine's studio, I had to jump right in. "I know this is a cliché, but it does seem so much worse because she was so young, and had everything going for her. Wasn't she even about to win the graduating student award?" Agnes was on the faculty committee for the award, and I knew she would have heard the same whisperings I had.

"Samantha, you know I can't really say. We hadn't come to an official decision yet," Agnes said. "But yes, Catherine was certainly near the top of the list. We all admired the progress she'd made this year."

I took a long gulp of coffee, pretending to mull this over, while she had really just confirmed what I already thought.

"Who do you think is next in line? I know you can't really say," I said the moment she looked up at me with a warning glance. "But I obviously don't have anything at stake in it this year. I'm just curious to know who might have a good chance at winning now." *Now that Catherine was out of the way*, I didn't say.

"Well, you know it's a strong group this year," Agnes replied, considering. "I personally think Chris Waters or your friend Benny both have a good chance at winning. Possibly Jessica Brown, I don't know if you know her?" I confirmed that I did not know her particularly well, but thought she was one of the other women in Catherine's studio space. Chris, of course, I did know, she of the long legs and crocodile smile.

"How much is the award this year?" I asked. There had been an announcement about a major new donor recently, though the administration hadn't yet said how scholarships or awards might change.

"It's wonderful, really, with the new donation that's come in. We'll be able to award fifteen thousand dollars this year. It's the first time it's been that much, ever." Agnes beamed.

I made some encouraging murmurings in agreement, while thinking that this might be my first big breakthrough. In past years, the award was around five thousand dollars. I might be poor, but even I didn't think that was quite enough to kill for. Fifteen thousand, on the other hand, could seem like a lot to someone who has nothing. At least I could cross Benny off the list of award-related suspects, since he was probably the last person here to need money that badly.

We finished our lunch in amicable silence, Agnes making promises to bring me an exhibition catalog to class on Friday for a new sculpture show she thought I would like, before she left for her afternoon class. We parted ways, with her on her way back to the sculpture rooms, while I walked one floor up to the library.

I had held various work-study positions since I'd started school, and as much as I had loved the darkroom, my job now in the library was probably my favorite. It was in an older, less recently renovated part of the building, with the same skylights as the rest of the top floor. In late afternoon when I worked, sunlight would pour in, highlighting the dust motes that swirled between stacks of books. It was a beautiful collection, all old art books and artist monographs: huge, oversized books of paintings and small books of Greek antiquities and new books full of impenetrable essays on contemporary art. Even if I didn't have to work, I could easily spend hours in the stacks, seated on the green carpeting with piles of books around me, flipping through artwork all afternoon.

When I got to the library that afternoon, I said my hellos

to the library staff (another older woman in the Agnes style and one younger man who had graduated a few years before) and to the two students coming off their shift, before rolling out the cart of books to be reshelved. While others may see it as a basic chore, I honestly love reshelving books. It's the best way to get to know all the different sections of the library, since the students before you might have looked at books you'd never even think to pick up. *Welding Techniques for the Beginner*, say, or *Religious Tapestry of the Middle Ages*. I tried to put aside my lunchtime conversation and let my mind wander while I reshelved, a peaceful twenty minutes without having to think about Catherine.

But, of course, the moment I took my seat behind the front desk, my thoughts returned to her once again, and to the books I had seen in her studio. I casually looked over my shoulder, into the staff offices. Both were engrossed in telephone conversations, the younger man answering an email at the same time. Coast pretty clear, in other words. I typed Catherine's name into the database system, pulling up her recent history and borrowing record. I wasn't technically supposed to do this, as it was an invasion of privacy and all that. But at the moment, I didn't think Catherine would particularly mind.

I scrolled back through the books she had taken out over the past few weeks. It seemed like I was right about her taking a sociology or legal studies class: after winter break, her record was full of books with titles similar to the one I had seen in her studio, all seemingly about legal questions around families. Maybe she was writing a paper about herself for class, something about questions of paternity? I wasn't sure what the legal implications would be of not having an officially confirmed father, but assumed this would be an appropriate topic for a legal studies class. Rebecca worked part-time in the registrar's office, so maybe I could find out if these were on the reading list for a class in another department.

I clicked back through another page of Catherine's borrowing history, getting to the weeks just before our winter break. At that point, it was just a list of painting books and a few course readers I knew were for a film class we had taken together, so this seemed to confirm my thinking that she was taking a new class that had just started this semester. I was just about to pull up the current course catalog, when a familiar face appeared at the front desk.

"Hi, Samantha," Chris said in a stage whisper.

I tried hard not to jump and managed a smile just in time. I should really practice these reactions in a mirror more often.

"Chris, hi. How are you?"

"Good, doing really good, actually," she said, leaning her elbows on the counter as if I had just invited her to sit, stay awhile, and tell me everything.

I leaned back as far as my chair would allow, trying to give her the universal signal that I wasn't interested in chatting.

"Just taking a break from the studio, I had to give my eyes a rest. You know how it goes …" She smiled one of her knowing smiles, which seemed to say that she was a professional who maintained a rigid work schedule, while I was a lowly library assistant and a junior at that.

Funny, but compared to talking with Agnes, I didn't feel the slightest hesitation about putting Chris on the spot.

"Yeah, I'm sure you must be working really hard right now. On the graduating students exhibit? I keep hearing your name mentioned for the year-end award," I said, widening my eyes to show how incredible I thought she was. It was hard not to roll them while my eyes were open that wide.

She looked up at me through her eyelashes, the very picture of humility.

"That's very sweet, thanks Samantha," she said, even though I didn't exactly compliment her. "I obviously don't know anything about the award, but of course it would be great to win."

"Especially since it'll be so much more this year," I said, egging her on.

"Exactly, what an amazing little nest egg to start out with," she replied. "I'd love to do some traveling over the summer, so the award would certainly go a long way towards that."

I nodded in agreement. So either I was the only one who had missed some big announcement, or Chris had had another way of finding out, but in any case, she clearly didn't need me to tell her that the award amount had gone up.

"Well, I'd better be going. Can't lose the rest of this light," she said, waving over her shoulder while she practically pranced out of the library.

I knew I shouldn't let my personal feelings about her get in the way, but I honestly would not be too disappointed if Chris had to be my number one suspect. Only if she had to. Like if, for instance, she had some kind of insider knowledge about a sizable prize she was in the running for, with only one person standing between her and what she probably already thought of as her money.

The afternoon shifts were always busy, the reshelving nearly endless. I was out with the cart once again, looking for the call number NC730.2 (drawing techniques), when I heard my name whispered just behind me. I spun around as quickly as the narrow stacks would allow, to see Michael, Catherine's ex, directly in front of me. Compared to Chris's stage whisper, Michael was nearly inaudible and I had to lean closer to hear what he was asking me. Unfortunately, he took this as an invitation to take another step closer to me.

"I said, did I see you coming out of Catherine's studio this morning? I didn't know the police were allowing people back in there now." He looked down at me intently, through a curtain of his shaggy brown hair.

Of all the conversations we could be having, this would probably not have been my first choice.

"I, uh. I was just in Benny's studio with him," I stammered, which in my whisper voice just made me sound asthmatic.

Michael didn't look convinced. "So they are letting people in there now?" he asked again.

"I guess so," I said. "No one stopped me, obviously. I think Benny's been working in there with no problem." I tried to take a step back but could already feel a few oversized books pressing into my back and calves. I was in the corner where two shelves met, with Michael blocking one aisle and the book cart blocking the other. I looked down and noticed he wasn't holding any books, and still had his backpack on. So was he here to work, or was he just here to ask me intimidating questions at close range?

"Why do you need to get into the studios so badly?" I asked.

Michael was also a senior, but his studio was in a separate room on the other side of the building.

"I lent Catherine a few books just before she died," he replied. "I was hoping to get them back now."

Suddenly, it was obvious how tired he was, how what I saw as an intimidating grimace was really just exhaustion, underlined by the dark circles rimming his eyes. Still, I fought off this small wave of sympathy. What if this was just another weak excuse, like my supposedly missing pencil?

"What books were they?" I asked. "I could keep an eye out the next time I go in." To see Benny, that is. Definitely not to investigate any further.

"A couple of painting books, one on painting from photographs, one a Gerhard Richter monograph," Michael said. "I can grab them myself, but I wasn't sure the studios were open yet."

I nodded and murmured in agreement, and in what I thought signaled an end to this conversation. But Michael leaned against the bookshelves next to him, taking off his backpack and tossing it down. I guess we weren't quite finished yet.

We had never been close, but had been in enough classes together and seen enough of each other when he was dating Catherine that I guess he felt like I was someone it would be fine to casually corner in the library and hold as a conversational hostage.

I sighed. "What's wrong, Michael? I wouldn't have thought you'd be upset so about a few missing books."

His grimace only deepened, and I instantly regretted how harsh my question seemed. Come on, Sam. Nancy Drew would never be this mean.

He didn't answer immediately, instead pausing to take off his beanie and run a hand through his hair, brushing it out of his eyes. He slid his hands into his pockets and gave a tight, small shrug.

"I mean, what do you think? I miss Catherine," he said, finally making eye contact again. "We had just started talking again in the few weeks before … when we got back from winter break.

I just, I mean …" He trailed off.

With all his bluster and pomposity in classes, I had never seen him stammer like this. For a second, I could see how Catherine might be attracted to this other, more open and vulnerable side of Michael.

I didn't say anything, just put down the book I was holding and reached out to lay a hand on his arm. We stood like this for a few seconds before I said, "I hadn't realized you guys were speaking again lately. Catherine hadn't mentioned anything to me."

Michael nodded. "Yeah, we were just friends. We weren't getting back together or anything like." A bit of his usual bravado seemed to come back into his voice, his volume rising.

Was he just being adamant about their relationship status? Or was Michael trying to cover up the plaintive tone I could still discern, doing his best to brush off any sentiment I might read into his words? It was a good try, but everything about his posture and exhaustion indicated it was probably the latter – that he was in fact pretty devastated right now.

"Well," I said, trying to go for a more sympathetic approach. "I know your relationship really meant a lot to Catherine." I dropped my hand from his arm and picked up my books again, turning slightly to the cart to indicate I really had to move on. "If you ever want to come over and talk about it, about Catherine and everything, I mean, you'd be welcome to. I know Rebecca would be happy to talk, too," I said in one last burst of inspiration.

I could just see it now: Michael, slightly drunk and opening up to me, revealing some damning fact that could only point to him as the killer. Great idea, Sam. Just remember, that would mean you're standing in the library being cornered by a murderer right now.

"Really, I mean it," I said, and started to push the cart towards the end of the stack.

Michael just nodded and mumbled a thanks, finally picking up his bag and turning to go. I was about to breathe a sigh of relief when he turned back, his face and tone suddenly transformed back to its usual, permanently smirking self.

"Oh, and really Sam, if you're going to poke around in Catherine's things, don't be so obvious about it. I'm sure I wasn't the only person to see you there." With that, he gave a little snide wave and walked off, leaving me frozen in the aisle.

What the hell was that? I fought off the urge to silently scream in my head, and looked down at the book still in my hand. Okay, put the book on the shelf, Sam. Move the cart. Walk back to the desk. I followed my own instructions woodenly, walking stiffly back to the desk and sliding onto the high chair at the counter.

I checked out books for the few students who were waiting, working on autopilot. It was hard to decide how shaken up I should feel right now. Was Michael telling me to be careful for my own sake? As far as I knew, news of the police's theories and the actual facts of Catherine's death were still in short supply. He might very well assume she had been killed, and didn't know anything about any supposed suicide. On the other hand, what if he was warning me off for a very specific reason? Like, that he knew exactly who'd killed Catherine and didn't want me to get too close to them? And by *them*, I mean to *him*. In other words, he could be nice and well-meaning, or scary and murderous. My shift couldn't end fast enough.

Chapter Six

Thankfully, I was able to sneak out of the library a bit early. A couple hours later, I was seated at the Phans' dining table, slurping noodles to drown out the sound of Stephanie lecturing me about how ridiculous it was that I thought I could solve a murder better or faster than people whose job was to do exactly that.

Luckily, there was nothing that made me feel better than a hot bowl of kuy teav, a soup that Steph's mom made on the regular. It was essentially the Cambodian answer to chicken noodle soup, but way better than any that my mom ever made. My mom is good at many things, but most often dinner came from a can or the freezer, and certainly didn't include things like fresh lemongrass or chili oil, which I was now pretty certain was something I couldn't live without.

I was so busy with the noodles that I didn't hear anyone walking up the stairs until the door was opening, and Arun was walking in. I hastily wiped my mouth with the first thing I could see, which unfortunately was just the back of my own hand. I put down the spoon, like I was a civilized person who didn't inhale huge bowlfuls of soup.

"Arun, hey!" I said. I was always amazed at how much my

voice could betray me, coming out in a rusty squeak like I was the Tinman, except, instead of not talking to anyone, I really just couldn't talk to Arun.

"Hey, Sammy," he said easily, coming in and sitting down across from me. Arun shrugged off his jacket and reached over to Stephanie's bowl, plucking off a piece of chicken while she scowled. "What's going on with you guys?"

"Samantha thinks she's Nancy Drew," Steph answered before I could say anything. She wrapped her arm protectively around her bowl, hunching over it like a beleaguered younger sibling who was never given anything to eat, despite the reality that she was everyone's favorite and knew it. The Phans were all wonderful, but her parents had still not quite forgiven Arun for leaving school. When I'd first met him, he was studying journalism at a college downtown, but he left when an entry-level job came up at *The Boston Globe*. Somehow, he had convinced the paper to hire him, catapulted by a professor who'd mentored him, but couldn't convince his parents that it had been the right move.

Now, I could feel my cheeks turning a bright red. "Not Nancy Drew," I said, shooting Steph a warning look. "It's just, no one really knows what happened to Catherine. I mean, the police just seem to be going in the wrong direction, and all we ever hear is gossip. I just want to get to the bottom of it, to know what really happened." I hoped this sounded reasonable and not like I was a child playing police dress-up.

To my relief, Arun was looking at me thoughtfully, nodding.

"I'm sorry," he said evenly. "That must be really difficult. Of course you'd want to know what happened."

"Thank you," I said, trying to glare at Steph, who refused to meet my eye. "And it's not like I'm running around doing crazy stunts. It's just a lot of talking to people, looking around."

"Looking around a crime scene," Steph said. "Talking to people who might have killed someone."

Yes, okay. That was another way to look at it. But Arun, bless his journalist's heart, didn't look like this was a ridiculous prospect.

"So what have you done so far?" he asked.

"Well, I really only got started this morning. Going through Catherine's studio, looking through her things there," I said.

Now that someone else seemed to be taking this seriously, someone who didn't even know Catherine or have anything at stake here, I suddenly felt a bit unsure. Not about what I wanted to do, but about what I'd done so far. Did some snooping and a few conversations really add up to all that much?

"I didn't find anything particularly new or out of the ordinary there. But I was interrupted by our friend Benny, who also works in that studio suite. So I guess I might need to go back?" I said, hating the way my voice ended in a question.

"I think you may have to tell me more about who's involved first. I obviously know you and Rebecca from the store, but I'm not sure I even met Catherine more than a couple times," Arun said. "She was the blond girl who was always with Benny?"

I proceeded to go through a who's who of the people around Catherine, starting with those of us closest to her: Rebecca and her sympathetic tutting; Benny and his stoic demeanor; Mel and all her gossip.

"Honestly," I said, "I feel like I'm laying out a Clue board here. I know it's implied in the fact that I'm trying to investigate, but the second you start talking about people like this, it seems like everyone becomes a character." For the sake of fairness, I should even put myself in the game. I could just picture the caricature that would be on my playing card: upswept curly ponytail and round glasses, perpetually messy or just forgotten makeup. If I was being generous, I would have said I looked like an arty Liz Lemon. If I was being honest, I would probably just focus on the messy part.

"I know," Arun was saying. "It's the same in any story I do: you always wind up creating a cast of characters. The best you can do is try to treat them fairly, consider them objectively. They can be people with characteristics, not just characters."

"Tell him about the ex-boyfriend," Steph cut in. She had finished dinner but was still sitting with us, idly fidgeting with her hair and adding the occasional remark about each person. I had texted her the details of my conversation (or confrontation?) with Michael immediately after it had happened.

"Last year, Catherine was with this guy, Michael. Tall, brown hair, lanky. I guess he was nice enough – I mean, he obviously had to be to her – but I've been in classes with him a few times. He's the kind of guy who always has to be the loudest, make the biggest work, you know?" I said. I wanted to be fair, but especially after his closing remark in the library, it was hard to feel motivated to paint a rosy picture of Michael. "I talked to him a bit today, and he mentioned that he and Catherine had started talking again recently. In the last few weeks before she died."

"Did they have an especially bad break up?" Steph asked. "I can't remember."

"I don't think so," I said. "Not really. They had been together for maybe six months, and it sounded like Catherine was just ready to move on. I think she was tired of all his macho crap and wanted a quieter senior year."

"So why start talking to him again?" Arun asked. "Did Catherine often have on-again, off-again kind of relationships?"

No, she didn't, and I said as much. Unfortunately, this was the exact kind of relationship that Arun seemed to be in. In the few years I'd known him, he had broken up and gotten back together with the same woman countless times, someone he'd known since high school. Every time they broke up, I would let myself get my hopes up, just for a moment. Only to have them come crashing back down, every. single. time. I was never fast enough to tell him how I felt in the moment, too afraid to find out he only saw me as his little sister's friend, or, even worse, like a surrogate younger sibling myself. Steph provided the occasional update, so I knew that now was one of those times when Arun was single. Unfortunately, what this usually meant for me was that I had an even harder time than usual talking to him like a regular person, and not a person who was petrified and awkward. In my defense, I'd like to see you take in his sharply cut black hair, chiseled jawline, and perfectly worn-in denim jacket, and not turn into a stammering mess yourself.

"Maybe Michael was angry that they weren't getting back together," Steph said. "Maybe very angry."

I gasped theatrically. "Look at you, supplying motives! See, I knew you'd come around eventually."

She rolled her eyes. "It's easy to dislike him. And it's easy to see him doing something impulsive and making a huge, awful gesture like this."

Steph definitely had a point. As much as I didn't want to think that I had been cornered by a murderer today, this was as good a motive as anything I could come up with. But, as I reminded them, we couldn't just go around accusing people because we didn't like them. I told them about my conversation with Chris.

"She didn't need me to tell her about the award money," I said. "And honestly, pretty much anyone could guess that Catherine would be first in line this year, or at least the most serious competition. She won a smaller award last year within the painting section, so it seems safe to assume she'd be at the top again. I don't know if it's really enough money to kill for, but I could see someone being desperate for fifteen grand."

The pair agreed, Arun making a comment about greed being one of the oldest motives in the book. I hesitated before I continued.

"There may be one other possibility," I said. "This year, Catherine was working closely with this professor, Professor Thompson. Every senior works with a couple of advisors, like mentors? So she was spending a lot of time with him lately."

"And?" Arun prompted me. "Is he some professor everyone hates?"

"Not exactly," I replied, looking at Steph and willing her to understand without my having to spell it out.

She nodded slowly, turning towards Arun. "Remember that math teacher in high school who resigned, but really everyone said he got fired for hitting on a student?"

"Ah," Arun said, comprehension dawning. It wasn't that abuse was hard to talk about, actual or potential or just rumored about. But it was hard to say out loud that my friend might have been a victim of this abuse.

"So if Catherine had turned him down, or threatened to go to the dean or something like that, then I could see Thompson having a pretty good reason to … to want to avoid that," I said. "Of course, this is assuming he did something wrong in the first place. I'm not some big fan of his, but I also don't want to make assumptions based on gossip. Catherine never said anything about him bothering her, but, you know. We've heard enough stories about other students to know that people rarely choose to come forward and do anything about him. Whatever he does or doesn't do, I've never heard of there being anything like official evidence against him."

"Is there any way you can talk to him about this?" Arun asked, earning a swat on the arm from Stephanie.

"Listening is one thing," she said. "But we don't need to encourage her to seek out more potential murderers to have close, private conversations with."

Just when I thought Steph was finally coming around to my side.

"I was actually thinking I'd try to see him tomorrow," I said, jerking my arm away before Steph could hit me, too. "I could say that I'm starting to think about next year, and wanted to talk about working together, with him as my mentor."

Steph glared at me but didn't protest any further.

"You know, if it helps, I could call the police tomorrow also. As press," Arun said. My eyes lit up and he put a hand up to caution me. "I can't guarantee that they'll tell me anything new. But I could at least see if there are any additional details they'd be willing to release."

"That would be great," I stammered, doing the squeaky Tinman voice again. "Yeah, thank you so much. I guess just call me if you hear anything?"

"You got it," he said, standing to go, giving Steph's hair a ruffle as he headed to his room. She stared me down.

"What?" I said, feigning innocence.

"I said you should tell my brother you like him," she hissed. "Not try to get close to him by investigating a murder."

What can I say? I never was very good at flirting.

Chapter Seven

Sitting in class the next morning, I tried to figure out what exactly I'd say to Professor Thompson. When I had gotten home from dinner last night, I'd emailed him to set up a meeting today during his office hours, writing that I was getting ready for next year and wanted to talk about senior advisors. Now the question was, how was I going to segue from that to Catherine?

The classroom was dark, the projector playing a documentary about *Godzilla* (the 1954 original, since this was a film history class called, appropriately, Flash Bang: Film and Media of the Atomic Age). Around me, everyone showed the same signs of struggling to wake up: coffee cups out on every desk, sweatshirt hoods up to hide slowly closing eyes, and at least one person who just blatantly put their head down. I couldn't take my phone out in the dark room, so I hunched over my open notebook, trying to see my notes in what little light there was. So far, all I had was a simple word map with Catherine written at the top and circled, then an arrow to the side pointing to Thompson's name and a note that read, *Time spent together?* Great start, Sam. The simplest approach in this meeting would be to play the gushing groupie, tell Thompson what great things

I'd heard about him from Catherine, say I was so excited to work with him, etcetera. But I didn't know Thompson well enough to know whether bringing up Catherine's name alone would be enough to prompt him to talk about her, or if I would really need to pry. Well, I thought, I'd find out soon enough. I did my best to jot down a few more words in my notebook, then gave up and tried to focus on the explanations of the allegorical meanings in *Godzilla*.

At noon on the dot, I was walking down to the second floor and into Professor Thompson's office. Faculty offices were usually in the back of the building, past the classrooms and studios. Like the suites of senior studios, most faculty were in large rooms with modular cubicles set up. I guess most were expected to have their own studio spaces or otherwise meet with students in the cafe downstairs or the library. Also like the seniors, the faculty too seemed split between those who kept their offices as austere white spaces, calm and empty, and those who tried to create a home away from home feeling, with a cluttered array of chairs and pillows.

Professor Thompson was the latter. His office was at the very back of the room, crammed with books and art knick-knacks on shelves lining the back wall, with a minimalist matte white Rachel Whiteread cube next to a glossy ceramic clementine covered in mold, that I recognized as the work of a younger artist I followed on social media. I knocked on his part of the partition as I stuck my head into his cubicle.

"Hello, come in! Samantha, right?" His voice seemed far too loud for the small space as he gestured for me to take a seat next to his desk.

Thompson himself was seated in a mid-century modern

office chair, all ergonomic back support in black and chrome, at a simple blond wood desk with an open laptop out. Pinned to the wall in front of his desk was a series of black-and-white photographs, eight-by-ten images of movie stills, Cindy Sherman photos, and at least one reproduction of a painting I didn't recognize, that showed a man in a bathrobe shaving, floating in a spotlight against a solid black background.

"That's right, it's Sam." I smiled, sinking into the small armchair he'd offered.

Its black leather was so smooth, I was afraid I'd slide right off if I moved around too much. I settled for both feet planted on the floor, like I was confident and meant business, but open and relaxed at the same time, and definitely not about to slip off the chair. You couldn't help but wonder what kind of signal this chair choice was meant to send. In contrast, Agnes's cubicle had been designed like a sleek therapist's office, with two cushy (and equal) chairs that actually invited long conversation, the kind where you could move around without fear of suddenly falling to the ground.

"So, Sam, what can I do for you?" Thompson was looking at me expectantly, and in that moment, I saw why he got away with so much of what he did.

Even if half of what was said about him was wrong, the other half was still a lot to have to excuse. But the way he was looking at me now, with cool blue eyes that seemed to say I was the only thing he ever wanted to look at again, well. I could see how an ability like that could take someone far – like an artsy, younger Bill Clinton.

"Well, as I think I said in the email yesterday, I'm starting to plan for my senior year. So I wanted to talk about maybe getting set up with you as my advisor for next year?"

Thompson grinned, as if all he wanted in the world was to be my advisor, like I wasn't one random student in a sea of a couple hundred whom he had never heard of before. "Of course, of course. I'm happy to talk about that. What kind of work are you planning to focus on?"

"Well, I mainly work in sculpture now, doing a lot of work with Agnes – Professor Pinel?" I wish I didn't sound so nervous, but it was hard to keep the stammer out of my voice when faced with those cool blue eyes. Thompson nodded at me encouragingly. "And I think I will continue to focus on sculpture next year, but I do have some experience with painting, and wanted to incorporate more painting into my sculpture work, which is why I thought of you." I paused, hoping he wasn't going to ask for more details about this imaginary work.

"Of course, that sounds great," Thompson beamed. "Have you set up another advisor yet?"

"No, you're the first professor I've talked to about this," I replied. I figured there was no reason to wait to lay it on, the thicker the better.

And it was clearly the right approach, met immediately by an indulgent, even knowing, smile from Thompson. He woke up the laptop and tapped away for a moment before responding. "So I do still have a few spots left open for next year. I try to limit my senior mentees to a dozen or so." He looked at me expectantly, apparently needing me to validate the idea that, yes, he was so good he shouldn't be held to the same standards of other professors who were usually required to work with up to twice as many students. I smiled and nodded.

Thompson half closed the computer and turned his full attention back to me.

"That said, working with me does have its challenges. I expect a lot from my students. We would certainly be meeting more often than most other advisors require. I like frequent check-ins, and I stay on top of progress." As he spoke, his voice somehow becoming more commanding in tone in a way I could only dream of emulating, he stretched one leg out and crossed the other over it. With the way that he had turned towards me, this meant that his left leg was now solidly resting against my ankle.

I froze. What was ever the right answer in this situation? Move my ankle and risk alienating Thompson so early in the conversation? Or leave my leg where it was and send the wrong idea? In this case, if I wanted to get close to him and understand his relationship with Catherine, I was afraid it would have to be the second option. I doubled down on the charm offensive.

"Absolutely, I understand. And I think that level of commitment would definitely be worth it," I said. "After all, I heard such great things about you from Catherine. I know she loved working with you."

He seemed momentarily taken aback at the mention of her name, but quickly recovered. Still, in that split second I thought I could see the way that his eyes could switch from calm and cool to icy and hard in an instant.

"Yes, Catherine was great to work with. A very talented student."

I waited for him to continue.

"I didn't know you two were so close."

"Oh yes," I said, still gushy. "Everyone loved Catherine. I just can't believe some of the things I've been hearing about her, like from the police and stuff? It just all seems so unbelievable."

Was it just my imagination, or did Thompson finally move

his leg away from me only at the mention of police and rumors? I shifted in my chair, struggling to keep an open mind.

"Of course, it's a terrible tragedy," Thompson said, though he didn't seem willing to say anything further.

"Were you two very close?" I asked. "I know how easily that happens with advisors, especially in the stress of senior year."

Thompson frowned for a moment, then seemed to shake it off. His eyes brightened again, as if the cool, calm, and collected charm switch had been flipped back on.

"Catherine was a talented painter, a great student. It's always a pleasure to work with such dedicated, creative young artists."

I smiled, mumbling something between an agreement and a thank you. "I guess I have just one other question, to go back to the meetings you were talking about? About how often should I count on meeting with you next year?"

"Well, I like to meet with all my students once a week for a quick check-in, and then do a longer studio visit once a month, possibly twice if you're running into difficulties." He smiled, reassuring and in charge, as if I'd be completely fine in life if only I talked to him once a week.

"Okay, great, that sounds great," I said. It did sound great, and nothing at all like Catherine's schedule.

I would have to check with Rebecca, but as far as I knew, Catherine had been seeing Thompson two or three times a week. And it hadn't sounded like they were quick check-ins either, but studio or office visits stretching the whole lunch hour. I was just about to ask another question, and mention Catherine's name to see if I could get his eyes to do the creepy switch again, when a boy with long hair and an orange baseball cap stuck his head around the corner, saying a low hello to Thompson.

"Well, Sam, it was great meeting you," Thompson said, giving me one of those awkward two-handed handshakes. "Just email me to confirm the details for next year."

With one final smile, that was my cue to go.

I gathered up my bag and coat, and walked out, not stopping until I was downstairs in the lobby. I paused at a bulletin board, pretending to look at the various flyers for gallery talks and new shows. Benny had already been here, leaving one of his bright pink signs for the mental health event right in the middle of the board. I sighed. I wasn't quite sure what I had learned from talking with Professor Thompson. Except, of course, that he'd seemed to meet with Catherine far more often than he did with other students. And I know that the leg thing wasn't enough to prove anything, nor was it his fault he had particularly piercing blue eyes. All the same, his demeanor was certainly starting to add a ring of truth to everything I'd heard about him.

I made a mental note of the date and time on Benny's flyer and continued across the lobby, heading up yet another musty staircase to the sculpture studio on the second floor. There was no class held there on Thursday afternoons, so those of us taking "Mud, Mineral, Clay" were free to use the facilities. Whether it would help me think through everything or not, I did need to work on my miniature pottery for tomorrow's class.

I dropped my bag on the floor next to a workbench, and headed to the back of the room to pick up my small urns, again lining them up on the bench with my various pots of glazes and paints. So far I had a set of six urns that had made it through the firing process without breaking, all under three inches in height. Each was a classic amphora shape (although not all the handles had survived the heat of the kiln). Now, each one would need to be painted, with tiny Grecian figures added to circle each form in bands of terracotta and black. I heaved a heavy stack of books out of my bag that I had picked up at work the day before: *History of Ancient Pottery: Greek, Etruscan and Roman; Greek Pottery Painting; Greek and Roman Pottery and Small Terracottas.* So just some light reading, all with plenty of pictures to work from. I flipped open to a few pages I had already bookmarked, showing full color spreads of classic Greek motifs of athletes and revelers styled in red and black. To start, I would have to paint each urn in a dark brown umber, which would turn even darker and more velvet when it was fired. I always felt a bit like an alchemist at this stage in the pottery studio, forever in awe of the way that simple mixtures of minerals could transform from something humdrum and blah to a shining, vibrant color.

Quickly, I felt my mind calm and settle with each dip of the paintbrush into the pot of glaze, each swipe of paint along the smooth pottery. This kind of work was always my favorite: with no small or intricate details to worry about yet, I could simply make something, let my hands take over, be in my zone. Still, as I built up the layers of thin glaze, I felt my mind start to wander back to Professor Thompson and our conversation. I wasn't sure what to make of his reluctance to talk about Catherine. Everyone else I talked to, whether they really knew her or not, seemed almost bizarrely or inappropriately eager to talk about her death, as if we were all living on the set of a true crime show now and everyone wanted equal camera time. But Thompson clearly didn't, and he didn't strike me as someone who would be particularly modest in this (or any) situation. So obviously, the conclusion I had to come to was that he had something to hide. That they were much closer than they should have been, for instance. I couldn't quite see Catherine being drawn in by him, but I knew it had happened. It was too easy for people like Thompson, who could use whatever charisma they might have, bolstered by their position of power over everyone around them, especially when those people were just young and eager to get ahead. And if something had happened between them, something that went south, what would Catherine have done? She had a strong conscience and seemed to always know what to do, not relying on everyone else's opinions to guide her. So would she have threatened to go to the dean or otherwise expose Thompson? But if she had, I couldn't see her waiting around to act or even telling Thompson about her plans in advance. I paused my painting long enough to rub my eyes in exhaustion. Unfortunately, the only person who could answer such a practical problem so well would have been Catherine.

There was also the question of means, which I maybe, just maybe, might have overlooked so far. Just slightly. Would Thompson even have known that Catherine was diabetic? Or that a large enough dose of insulin would be fatal for her? Catherine wasn't shy about disclosing her diagnosis, but she also didn't go out of her way to broadcast the fact. And it didn't factor into her art, her paintings, as far as I had ever seen, so I couldn't see it coming up naturally in a critique.

I was startled back to earth by a woman striding through the open door, her high-heeled boots noisy on the rough studio floor. She tossed her bag down at the workbench next to me, and perched herself on the tabletop one row over.

"Hiya, Sam-o," Ricky said.

Why is it that people with the shortest names are plagued by the most variations and nicknames?

"Hiya, Ricky," I replied, giving her a curt smile.

Ricky had been living with Benny and Catherine since the start of the school year, along with another student, a boy named Dan. The four of them rented an apartment much closer to school (and much nicer than the triple-decker apartment Rebecca, Mel, and I split), in a small apartment building that bordered a nearby park. They hadn't had to do much when they'd moved in, electing to decorate the clean white walls minimally, pooling their (not insubstantial) funds to furnish the place from a design store downtown. In contrast, Rebecca and I had spent a full week sanding down the decades of rough plaster and paint that had built up on our walls before we could paint them back to a calm neutral greige-and-white scheme. In any event, I knew Ricky pretty well, since she'd seemed to be around a lot whenever I was over with Benny and Catherine.

"What's going on?" I asked her now.

"Oh, you know. Usual everything," she said, swinging her feet. "Have to finish that set of vases before tomorrow's class. You?" I gestured to the urns arrayed in front of me, replying that I was doing the same.

"Of course, the cute minis!" Ricky squealed.

I managed a smile through my clenched jaw. Don't get me started on the idea that all miniatures have to be cute, that they can't be functional or spooky or contain any kind of violence or be historically accurate. I made a mental note to text Ricky an article about Francis Glessner Lee and her miniature crime scenes. On the other hand, maybe she really didn't mean "cute" as an insult. After all, this was a woman who made big, bulbous vases that were decorated as if they were extravagant layer cakes.

She was just walking back to the bench now with one, putting it up on a decorating stand so it could be easily rotated while being painted. "Hey, I wanted to let you know, we're actually having a party tomorrow night," she said. "At our place. For my birthday. So you'd be totally welcome to come."

"Oh, happy birthday! I didn't realize. Yeah, that sounds nice. I'll try to come over."

Although, already I could see Rebecca's apoplectic reaction, her enraged muttering about how it was far too soon for a party, any kind of party, and especially one at Catherine's apartment. Even if Benny himself had signed off on it.

"Great! It's '90s television themed, so pull out your best Carlton sweater!"

"Yeah, I'm not gonna do that," I replied. "I was always more of a Blossom girl myself."

It was true that my parents had almost named me after Mayim Bialik. It was also true that as a white kid (and one too young to have seen *The Fresh Prince* when it was originally on), Carlton would probably not be the best costume pick for me.

Ricky shrugged and turned to her vase, getting ready to add the porcelain "frosting" she was so attached to. I watched while she filled up a piping bag with some kind of gloopy air-dry clay, using the regular kind of nozzle you would frost a cake with, and started to add a looping swirl around the rim of the vase. Maybe I was overthinking this, but perhaps there was a reason she was forging ahead with this party so soon after Catherine's death. Maybe she wasn't too upset that Catherine had died. Maybe beneath that bubbly, frothy surface was a person who could get rid of someone if they simply didn't like them enough. And if my concern about Thompson as a suspect was that he didn't have the means or knowledge about Catherine's diabetes to know how to commit this murder, that certainly wouldn't have been a problem for Ricky. Who better than someone she lived with to have access to Catherine's medications? Ricky could have tampered with the insulin at any time, then sat back for the perfect crime: Catherine would have died whenever she got to the tampered-with vial, a seemingly random tragedy.

Ricky looked up suddenly, catching me staring.

"It looks great!" I said only a little too loudly. "Love the swirls."

I turned back towards my books and urns, busying myself with cleaning off my paintbrush, ready to finish glazing another.

By urn six, I was flagging. My eyes had started to sting with tiredness, and I knew it wouldn't be long before my eyesight would start to blur altogether, turning the urn designs into a watery mess. I was almost finished with the base layer of glazes but still needed to go back and add in figures on half of them. The work bench was now scattered with quick pencil sketches of Greek figures, tracing paper laid out of the books so I could copy straight from the images, getting certain poses exactly right.

It was a relief when my phone started to buzz, only somewhat tempered by nerves when I saw that it was Arun calling. I threw Ricky an apologetic smile and headed into the hallway to take his call.

"Hey, Arun, how's it going? Yeah, thanks for calling me." In my two years of knowing him, had I ever managed not to speak this quickly?

"Hey, Sammy, it's going pretty well. It looks like I'm going to be up late tonight to make my deadline for tomorrow, but I guess most writers never learn, right?"

I could just picture his rueful smile, ever the cute procrastinator.

"But I did have time today to make that call to the cops who are on Catherine's case," Arun continued. "I spoke to the officer in charge of press, a guy called Pat O'Brien. I've run into him reporting on a few other cases in the past. He's an okay guy, clearly just doing the job, and you both know it's not his fault he can't disclose as much information as you may want."

I didn't say anything, just waited for him to continue while I paced in a tight circle at the end of the hallway, surrounded by closed doors and the low sounds of classes going on behind them. From the other end of the hallway, the sounds of someone hammering away floated through the open door of the woodshop.

"Yeah, I think you know what I'm going to say," Arun paused. "They're not releasing any new details about the case, definitely nothing you don't already know. Just the same information about the way she died, where she was found. That they're still following up a few leads."

"Well, thank you so much for trying. I really appreciate it," I said, getting ready to let Arun get back to his imminent deadline.

"Hang on, though, there was one thing that was pretty clear. O'Brien made it sound like the guys in charge were pushing for a quick close for this. They get pretty nervous about any bad coverage of the city's campuses. It sounds like they're looking to wrap up the case in the coming week. And they're likely to rule it accidental, like you thought."

"That's ridiculous. What, so a few concerned parents call the school and they think the best solution is to sweep Catherine's death under the rug?" I was instantly fuming, only slightly aware that my voice was rising more than it should be given the subject at hand. "How do they think that's going to help anything?" If nothing else, I guess it would at least give Benny's campaign a good starting point: no more cover-ups around student mental health.

"I know, I know. It's really tough. But you have to try to understand it from their perspective. There's no apparent murder weapon besides Catherine's own medication, that she probably had on her almost all the time. There was no sign of a struggle or anything stolen from her studio. The police are doing what they can to confirm it, but what they see is a person who died alone after making an understandable mistake." His voice dropped further. "Listen, I'm not saying you should give up. By all means, keep looking around. Maybe you'll find something the cops didn't after all. But you may have to seriously consider the possibility that Catherine's death really was an accident."

"You're right, it doesn't mean I should give up. Thanks, Arun."

In fact, what it really meant was that I would have to act even more quickly and figure this out before the police made a massive mistake.

"Hey, why don't you stop by for dinner again tonight? I think my mom is making lort cha – those noodles that you like."

Since when did Arun pay attention to my dinner preferences?

"Uh, thanks, yeah. That sounds great." This was me trying not to sound too surprised. "I may be late – I still have a bunch to get done in the studio here. But I'll text Steph later and see if it still works. And really, thanks again for making the call."

"Of course, Sammy, anytime. Happy to help."

I wasn't sure what surprised me more – that the cops thought

Catherine's case was almost closed, or that Arun remembered what noodles I liked.

Chapter Eight

Although it did take an inordinate amount of cajoling, Rebecca eventually agreed to go to the party with me the next night. And Mel, of course, who was immediately on board after making a broad proclamation about how this was exactly what "all of us" needed. The two of them had dressed as Scully and Mulder, because, as Mel put it, Rebecca's strawberry-blonde hair made the costume a "no-brainer." I really had to bite my tongue on that one. I'd stayed true to my Blossom inspiration and had pulled out a velvet hat and overalls. As embarrassing as this should probably be to admit, yes: I already owned the perfect outfit for this party.

Now, standing outside Benny and Ricky's building, I wished Blossom had been known for wearing large parkas. It was nine pm and the wind was howling down the narrow valley of their block, cold enough that no one else was outside, not even the hardiest of smokers. Mel hurried up to the door, pulling it open and gesturing to us to run in, but I reached out for Rebecca's arm, pulling her back.

"You go ahead, Mel," I called. "I just have to ask Rebecca something first."

Mel hesitated. She always liked to make a big group entrance, but eventually she shrugged, heading inside.

"Listen, I need to ask you something before we go inside. About Catherine." Well, not about *her*, exactly, but I didn't think Rebecca would wait for anything else right now.

"Go on," Rebecca said, hopping back and forth from one stockinged leg to another to keep warm. Really, why didn't they wear more coats on television?

"Okay, so I was thinking. About her insulin. You know how Catherine always kept everything in that little pouch? So she always had whatever she needed close by." I waited for Rebecca to nod before I went on. "Well, it occurred to me that if Catherine was killed because someone tampered with her medications, then whoever did it would have obviously had to have access to those medications. Even though she always had them on her." Again, I paused, hoping Rebecca would catch on without my having to spell it out, but still she hopped and waited. "The people who had the easiest access to her meds would be the people who lived with her."

"Oh, no," Rebecca said instantly. "Wherever this is going, I do not want to be involved. No. You can't think that Benny had anything to do with this." She shook her head. Between that and the hopping, she looked like a broken bobblehead, forlorn and insistent on someone's dashboard.

"No, not Benny. But hear me out: Catherine had two other roommates. Obviously they would have had the easiest access to her medications. So I think it makes sense to look around now, just to rule them out." I put my hands up, trying to placate her.

"Rule them out how?" Rebecca was always a pro at that kind of question, where her tone meant you were already being accused of the answer.

"I just want to look around Ricky and Dan's rooms. See if there's anything there that might show they had been through Catherine's things."

Since talking to Ricky yesterday, I had grown more and more suspicious of Catherine's roommates, if only because no one else would have had as easy access to her things. Surely if the medications had been tampered with, then whoever did it would still have a vial or syringe lying around. A murder weapon wasn't usually something you could just toss into the nearest trash can.

"No, absolutely not. I'm not going to help you invade their privacy. It was one thing to acknowledge that the police might be wrong, but this is totally different. If you think that either of them had anything to do with this, you should call that detective." Rebecca moved to walk past me, but I grabbed her by the arm again and wouldn't let go this time.

"Rebecca, come on. You know this is important. What does privacy matter compared to Catherine's death?"

Rebecca rolled her eyes at this. Okay, so not the right heartstring to tug on here.

"You wouldn't have to do any of the snooping yourself. Just help me distract Ricky and Dan so I can get into their rooms unnoticed. All you'd have to do is talk to them for a while. How bad can that be?"

"No, I'm not going to do it. I really think you should just talk to the cops. I'm not going to break into someone's room, and I'm not going to help you do it either."

With that, she pushed past me and into the building. I guess Blossom would have to go it alone.

Benny's apartment was on the top floor of a small brick

apartment building that had been refurbished about fifty years more recently than our building had been. Inside, the party was already in full swing, and I walked into blasting heat and people rapidly shedding outer layers. I smiled and shouted hellos to a few people I knew from school, waving at Ricky and mouthing a "happy birthday" at her. She apparently had taken her own suggestion and was wearing a Carlton-patterned sweater over a pair of short pink bike shorts, a glittery tiara topping it all off. I pushed through groups of people talking and dancing, making my way into the kitchen. I might have been dressed as a teenager, but I was definitely glad to be of drinking age at that moment.

Benny was holding court in the kitchen, in a huge brunette wig and an oversized jacket, trim pants combo, waving his drink around while he regaled a small group with what sounded like an anecdote about high school shenanigans in his small town. It looked like he was drinking a rum and Coke, and I hunted through the cabinets for a clean glass, finding the rum tucked behind a few packets of cookies.

I sidled up to him as the anecdote came to an end. "Elaine?" I shouted. It had to be either that or Fran from *The Nanny*.

"Of course, honey, you know I never miss an opportunity for a good pants suit." He grinned.

So, despite Rebecca's admonitions, it seemed it really wasn't too soon for a party after all. I hadn't seen Benny this relaxed for weeks.

"Mary-Kate or Ashley?" he asked, gesturing to my hat.

"Blossom," I said. Already I could tell that my voice would be gone by the end of the night. Nineties hip hop was blaring in the living room above the din of voices and people singing along. "Is Dan here, too?"

"Why do you want to know?" Benny grinned and nudged me with his elbow.

"Nothing like that, really. Just curious who's around."

"Sure, whatever you say. Yeah, he's here tonight. Pretty much everyone is." Benny was distracted then by a girl coming over with a slice of birthday cake, something pink and frothy-looking. I took the opportunity to slip away, and moved into the kitchen doorway where I had a clear view of the living room.

The lights were out, and the room was lit only by a few strands of fairy lights circling the ceiling, casting a pale glow on the makeshift dance floor. The sofa and coffee table had been pushed up against one wall and a small folding table brought out for a senior boy I recognized from Catherine and Benny's studio suite, who currently looked to be serving as DJ. His laptop cast more light than the strands of twinkle lights, and it was currently blasting a Destiny Child's song while about thirty people sang along, moving en masse to the beat. Rebecca and Mel were on the side of the room and whatever else I might have been annoyed by in the moment, even I had to admit that Scully and Mulder would always make a great couple.

Ricky was in the center of the floor, in a tight group with two other girls and Michael, Catherine's ex. She reached out to him, turning and blocking the other girls out of their little circle. I watched while she danced closer to him, putting his hands on her hips. It wasn't clear how much he was picking up what she was clearly laying down, but he also wasn't moving away.

They continued dancing as the next song came on, more Beyoncé that garnered a huge cheer from the room. Ricky seemed intent on staying close to him. Could I be looking at a motive in the making? If she was into Michael, and thought that he and Catherine might have been about to get back together, would she have been jealous enough to do something about it? Too bad the only help I had to snoop around her room was currently doing the "Single Ladies" dance with Mulder.

I continued walking around the perimeter of the room, dancing through the crowd over to the other door to the living room, which opened into a back hallway with two bedrooms and a bathroom. Benny and Catherine's rooms were on the other side of the apartment, both slightly smaller but with better light. I stopped momentarily at the front of the hall when I was pulled into a conversation about the relative merits of one brand of cigarettes over another, before I could extract myself and join the line for the bathroom.

With four people ahead of me, I was close to the door to Ricky's room. I leaned against it and rested my hand on the doorknob, pulling my phone out of my overalls pocket with the other hand, like I was just waiting and texting. Unfortunately, the doorknob wouldn't budge.

I should have known this wouldn't be so easy. If Ricky were anything like me, she would have stashed her things in some unused kitchen cupboard or under a potted plant before the party started.

I was about to dance my way back to the kitchen when Dan appeared in the living room door.

"Sammy-sam!" he yelled.

Maybe it was just this household that went for all the stupid nicknames.

"Dan!" I yelled back, smiling and trying to scoot past him. But he put his arm up on the wall, doing that move where you pretend to be casually leaning but really are blocking someone in. Great.

"How come I haven't seen you around lately? I miss our lunch smoke breaks."

One time. One time we'd shared a cigarette after lunch together and it seemed this had cemented something about our relationship for Dan.

"Just busy, working after classes and everything. You know how it goes." I was practically talking into his armpit, unsure how I could make it any clearer that I was trying to walk away.

"Well, I'm glad you're here tonight. Come dance," he said, reaching for my hand.

I pulled back as quickly as I could, pointing to my empty glass. "Have to refill first!"

I darted away and towards the kitchen, as quickly as the still-gyrating crowds would let me.

Benny was continuing to hold court in the kitchen, and it sounded like the conversation had moved from hometowns to impressions of various staff and teachers. I found the rum again and topped up my drink. (What? It was all for the case.) Making a show of putting the bottle away, I felt underneath the various packages of food, trying to find the key to Ricky's room. No luck.

Which made sense. I usually chose the least-used cabinet, something under the sink or farthest from the fridge. Cutting in loudly to Benny's conversation, I whipped off my hat with the energy of someone much drunker than I actually was.

"Benny! Remind me I'm leaving this here," I yelled, yanking open the cabinet beneath the sink. "Safer keeping!"

I was proud of the perfect slurred mistake I put into that, keeping it in a back pocket to regale Stephanie with later. Leaning down unsteadily, I took my time, as if I needed to find the perfect place for my hat. Tucked up in the front corner of the cabinet behind a pack of sponges was Ricky's phone and a set of keys. Bingo.

Finally, I was in Ricky's bedroom with the door shut, though the noise from the party was hardly dimmed. I didn't want to switch on the overhead light, so I was standing in the center of her room with my phone's flashlight turned on. Although she loved her decadently frosted vases, it seemed that Ricky kept her personal room pretty minimal – just a small twin bed and two white desks pushed together. There were no messy art supplies here or projects in process, all of which she must have kept at her studio in school. Instead, there were just a couple of piles of books on the desks and a large sketchbook, opened to what looked like notes on the glazing and firing process. In other words, everything was so minimal, there were no obvious hiding places.

But I had a suspicion we might be more similar than I'd initially thought. I pulled back the sliding door to her closet. Yep, stuffed full of all the things that would have messed up the view of her minimal space. Clearly Ricky was a proponent of my cleaning method, which was simply to throw everything into the nearest closet and shut the door.

There was no way I was going to have time to go through everything. At any moment, Ricky could go to check her phone and discover the keys missing. Or worse, bring Michael back here, leaving me to have to hide in the closet. I shuddered at the thought.

There was a small dresser, and I decided to start there, pulling open each drawer and rummaging through layers and layers of clothes: silky tops and ripped jeans, embarrassingly small underwear and unidentifiable garments covered in sequins. Realizing that I was digging blindly for what could potentially be a syringe, I pulled out a thick sweater and wrapped it around my hands, resuming my search now with the world's most awkward oven mitts.

Other than a bottle of ADD medication, I didn't find anything that wasn't clothes. Outside, a cheer went up and was followed by the sound of fifty people singing happy birthday. The line by the bathroom must have grown, too, because now I could hear voices directly outside the closed bedroom door. I would have to get out of here soon.

I knelt down in front of the dresser, reaching into the narrow space between the dresser and the wall for anything that might have fallen. No luck. I bent even closer to the floor and wiggled my arm under the dresser, still using my sweater-oven mitts. My hand brushed something bulky and I quickly pulled the sweater out so that I could grab the object, bringing out a small bundle of leaves. Okay, so Ricky liked to burn sage sometimes. I reached back under the dresser with my bare hand, and felt the smooth plastic edges of something about snapshot size. I pulled out three photos, shining my flashlight onto them: Michael. All three photos showed Michael, one in a classic social media selfie stance and two that were more casual images, with Michael caught unaware, laughing. Okay, so Ricky liked to burn sage sometimes and kept this sage with a pile of creepy stalker photos of Michael. Ordinarily, I might assume these objects were unrelated, just random items that had fallen off a dresser. But this was art school. Clearly, this girl was up to something witchy. I took a few phone pics of the photos and slid everything back under the dresser. No way was I going to disrupt whatever witchy thing was going on here. As far as I knew, I had a perfect record of not being the subject of other people's attempted magic, and I had no intention of ending that record now.

I shut the closet, giving the room a final once-over with my flashlight. I even ran my hands under her mattress, even though everyone knows that's the most obvious hiding place in the world. I waited for the voices in line to move down the hall, before slipping out the door and locking it behind me.

Okay, so no obvious signs of insulin-tampering in one room (except for some very apparent signs that Ricky had had designs on Catherine's ex-boyfriend, maybe soon-to-be boyfriend again, for who knew how long). But I would have to file that thought away for later, as there was still one more room to search. Mercifully, the hallway had cleared out, and I was able to get into Dan's room without any trouble. From the sounds coming out of the living room, it seemed like everyone was still being distracted by Beyoncé.

Dan, unlike Ricky, was apparently not a practitioner of our cleaning method. That is, it didn't seem like he had any cleaning method at all. The room was covered with clothes, and there were books and magazines on every surface. The closet door was open to reveal a dozen coats hanging over a huge pile of what had to be weeks' worth of laundry. Great move, Dan. Leave the closet open so girls know how gross you are before they make the mistake of doing anything with you.

I used my toe to nudge aside a stack of sweaters that was lying on a pile of books next to his bed. *Assemblage and Collage: A History* lay under a bright blue hoodie. So at least Dan had somewhat of an excuse for all the mess and assorted objects: I was sure everything here would make its way into a collage eventually, and I could see a few piles on the desk that had to be works in progress, with cardboard structures covered in all manner of images and textured materials. I played my flashlight over the rest of the desk, highlighting bottles of glue and paint pens strewn over various scraps of paper. I let the light linger on a stack of what looked like vintage *Playboy* magazines. A pretty gross look for him, but hardly illegal, I guess.

I stepped over half a dozen piles of stuff that looked like it had been found in the neighbor's trash can, making my way over to the closet. Forget obvious hiding places: here, Dan had endless hiding places. This was literally going to be looking for a needle in a haystack.

I was halfway done with sorting through his pile of laundry, checking the pockets of every pair of pants and sweatshirt for anything resembling a syringe or an insulin vial. So far, all I had found was a few gum wrappers, a set of earbuds, and two dollars in change (which I was keeping, thanks, although it hardly made up for the fact that I'd have to burn my hands off after touching all this junk). I dragged the tenth pair of jeans out of the pile and checked the back pockets. Nothing. But in the right front pocket, that tiny one that no one really knows what it's there for, there was something small and round. I pulled it out, silently praying for it not to be something extra repulsive. Instead, I was looking at a small pink piece of rubbery plastic, about the size and shape of a miniature bottle, with a lightly swirled design and an opening cut into the side.

At the sound of someone crashing down the hall, I hurried to get my flashlight off, shoving the object into my overalls pocket (and patting myself on the back for choosing a costume so suited for sleuthing). The door swung open, and Dan filled the frame, backlit by the suddenly bright lights of the hallway. He flipped the switch for the overhead light, to find me standing in the middle of the room, trying to pretend that I hadn't just almost vomited from the smell in his closet.

"Samantha! What brings you back here? Although I can't say I'm surprised."

I thought that leering was something they only did in movies from the 1950s, but apparently Dan had gotten the expression down perfectly.

I stammered, mumbling a few ums and ahs while I wondered how much time I had to come up with a believable excuse.

"It's okay, you don't have to make up some reason," he said, stepping closer to me. He didn't even bother to look down, apparently having memorized the topography of junk in the room. "I'm just glad to find you here."

"You … You are?" I said, trying to take a step back without tripping over anything.

"Of course," he said, reaching an arm out and pulling me towards him by the waist.

He was almost a whole foot taller than me, so I had to turn my face to avoid being smothered by his chest. Apparently he had gone with SpongeBob SquarePants to fit the party theme, having stapled a single yellow sponge to the middle of a white shirt. There was always that one guy.

He leaned down to kiss me and hardly seemed to notice when I turned my head away, nearly breaking my neck while leaning as far back as I could to avoid him.

"Let's go have that cigarette break first," I said, addressing the sponge. "I'm dying to smoke." And dying to get out of this room.

"Sure, whatever you say." I didn't think his leer could get

much worse, but still having his arm around me definitely didn't help matters. I cursed myself for not thinking to bring some kind of weapon with me. I mean, I didn't think I could get away with casually pepper spraying Dan, but what I wouldn't do for just one brass knuckle right now. Didn't even have to be a whole set.

I rushed out of the room, leading us through the living room where the party was now focused on a dance-off between Benny (Elaine) and Mel (Mulder). I practically leapt through the open window in the back of the room and out onto the fire escape.

Dan lit a cigarette and offered it to me. Even though I hated having to take anything that had been in his mouth and couldn't remember why I ever had before, I took a long drag on the cigarette, pretending to be fascinated by the building across the alley.

"You sure this is what you want?" he asked.

Yes, Dan, I would rather be standing outside in February with only overalls for warmth than be inside doing anything else with you. I smiled through my chattering teeth, nodding.

Mercifully, Rebecca chose that moment to poke her head out the window. "Sam, come in and dance with us." She was breathless, and had discarded her suit jacket at some point, now wearing a white tank top over her pencil skirt. Not very Scully, but still a good look for her. "Come on!" she yelled and ducked back into the living room, gesturing for me to join her.

"Sorry, I should really go in with her. I haven't done much dancing yet tonight." I handed Dan his cigarette back.

"It's okay, I'm sure they won't miss you that much."

"No, I should go in. Everyone's been so upset lately, it'll be good to have some fun with Rebecca."

I moved to go past him but he took a step sideways, blocking the window.

"Really? You're gonna be that girl? I thought you were fun, Sam." Dan glared down at me

Yeah, I was that girl, whatever the hell that meant. I never understood why guys thought getting mad was the way to get you to hook up with them.

"Come on, you don't have to make this a whole thing. Just let me go back in. We'll hang out soon, I promise."

"Whatever. You were the one in my room," he said, flinging down the cigarette and crushing it under his shoe. He stared down at me, tight-lipped, and for a moment I thought he wouldn't let me through. But after a few seconds too long, he stepped aside and I clambered back through the window, practically falling onto Rebecca.

Joining her and Mel to the dulcet tones of Mariah, I wondered about Dan's reaction. And I wondered why he had an insulin vial protector in the pocket of his pants. Because I had recognized that small pink item I'd found as one of a colorful set of insulin protectors that Catherine used, to help keep the vials from breaking in her bag. It might not have been the syringe itself, but it seemed damning enough. Ricky might have had some creepy photos of Catherine's ex-boyfriend, but at least she didn't have anything that had actually belonged to Catherine.

If you had asked me a few days ago if I thought Dan was capable of killing Catherine, I would have said absolutely not. He was annoying and kind of a jerk, but not particularly offensive. Now, I had to admit that his temper seemed worse than I'd thought. If Rebecca hadn't come along, would I have been able to get out of the situation? What if he had come on to Catherine and she rejected him? Could his temper be so bad that it had led him to murder?

Chapter Nine

Thankfully, the rest of the weekend was far less eventful than the party Friday night. Saturday, the three of us slept in before splitting off to our various jobs for the afternoon. The library was quiet on Saturday afternoons, so I was able to use the time to finish that now-overdue essay for my "Media of the Atomic Age" class. I ignored Benny and Mel's texts that evening, cajoling me to come out with them, and instead spent the evening tucked up in bed with an endless supply of grapefruit seltzer and sour cream and onion chips, falling asleep to a *Murder She Wrote* marathon. Best plans ever, I thought, only slightly doubting it when I eventually woke myself up by rolling over the bag of chips.

Perhaps because of this, I was more amenable the next night when Rebecca suggested we go out to dinner. I had spent the day in the studio at school, trying to tune up a new round of Grecian miniature urns based on last week's critique, but really just stewing over everything that had happened the previous week. When the police had first come to talk to me, I couldn't think of a single person who might have wanted to hurt Catherine, even if it was equally inconceivable that she might have hurt herself. Now, I suddenly had too many suspects. There was Thompson and whatever was keeping him from speaking about Catherine. And Chris, with the expensive travel plans that Catherine had stood in the way of. Now, it seemed I could also add Dan and his belligerence, and Ricky and her jealousy to the list, not to mention Michael, the object of Ricky's jealousy and himself someone with a prime motive for killing Catherine. If I wanted to keep a truly open mind, I should include the possibility that a random stranger had come in and attacked her, no matter how unlikely that seemed. I was beginning to feel like I couldn't see the forest for the trees. No amount of staring off into space in the studio was helping me figure out how I could narrow down the possibilities from here.

I tried to tune back into what Rebecca was saying, who so far had refused to discuss the case with me, thinking it wasn't right to listen to baseless speculation about her friends (and would probably be livid that I thought of it as a case at all. So much for her initial support, which I guess had only lasted until she'd realized what investigating involved). Also, it was hardly baseless speculation, I thought, but—

"Samantha. I said, are you going?" Rebecca was looking at me expectantly.

"To, um … Benny's rally?"

I took a wild shot in the dark that luckily received a curt nod.

"I think I have to work, sorry."

Not sorry. I loved Benny, but didn't love shouting crowds.

"I'm going to try. I have a big project due for my printmaking class in the afternoon tomorrow, so I'll have to see how far I can get in the morning." Rebecca paused, blowing lightly on a spoonful of soup and noodles to cool it.

Pho was the only good option in our neighborhood as the

temperatures crept down towards zero, so we were tucked into a red-pleather booth in the closest Vietnamese restaurant, huge bowls of steaming soup in front of us.

"What's going on, Sam? You're a million miles away."

"I know, I'm sorry. I'm just distracted thinking about Catherine still. I know I was only going to look into it lightly, just to try to get a sense of whether there was any better explanation other than her taking her own life. And now, I feel like I've found too many possibilities and it isn't any clearer than it was before."

I swirled my spoon through my bowl aimlessly, my head resting in my hand with my elbow propped up on the table: the very picture of dejection. I knew Rebecca would have limited patience with my moping, so I figured I should milk it while I could.

"Sam, I'm sorry. I know it hasn't been easy. But maybe now is the right time to go back to the police. Let them know what you've found and let them take it from there. You don't have to be the person worrying about this now. It's not your job." She reached across the table for my hand. "I wish Benny had been able to come tonight. The two of you need to distract each other."

But Rebecca was missing one crucial point: she should have remembered how much trouble I have letting go of problems. Like the time I disassembled and spent months reassembling one of the darkroom enlargers that had stopped working, not pausing until every last possible cause was ruled out. Or the time I covered our kitchen table with a thousand-piece puzzle of the Sistine chapel, coming close to tears any time someone suggested it might be time to move it, even though it had taken me months to finish it.

"I know, I know. Maybe I'll call the detective this week. I still have his card somewhere."

Rebecca smiled, giving me a pat before turning back to her soup. I had suddenly lost my appetite, and spent the rest of our meal twirling noodles in my bowl while listening to Rebecca describe the massive amount of work she had to get through for the printmaking project due tomorrow.

I let my mind wander even as we walked back to our apartment later, doing the classic Boston winter stance of head down, chin tucked into jacket, gloved hands tucked into pockets, and didn't come back to earth until my phone dinged. I pulled it out to see a text from Arun, asking how I was doing. I checked to see whether Rebecca had noticed, not wanting to explain the still confusing update in our friendship (now he apparently checked in on me?), but she was firmly in her own world, focused on putting one foot in front of the other down the icy sidewalk. I couldn't respond with my gloved hands anyway and slid the phone back into my pocket.

As we turned onto our street, I could see a light on in the window on our floor. "I thought Mel was out at work tonight?" I nudged Rebecca, gesturing up to our house.

"Maybe she got back early?" Rebecca replied, a mixture of hope and worry evident. "Or you could have just left a light on by mistake."

Although we both knew that Rebecca had drilled into me the importance of always turning off the lights enough times that I would never do this.

"Well, if someone's broken in, I think my leftovers are still hot enough to throw at them," I said, swinging my white plastic bag of takeout containers at her, but got only an unsteady smile for my efforts.

As we got to the top of our stairs, I gestured for Rebecca to hang back. But the door showed no evidence of having been broken into, at least none of the evidence that television shows have trained me to look for: no shattered doorframe here. So I just shrugged at her and slid my key into the lock, opening the door to a quiet apartment.

The door opened onto our front hallway, which had our bedrooms and living room just off of it. Mine was the room closest to the front, and the door was currently open, bright light spilling out. Still not speaking, the two of us took the few steps into my room together. My desk light was on, throwing a bright spotlight onto the wall, newly covered with rusty red graffiti: "YOU CAN'T SPELL PAINTING WITHOUT PAIN." The rest of the room was a mess of supplies and clothes, my dresser drawers each pulled and overturned, my supply boxes tipped over.

"What do you think, Rebecca? Should I toss my leftovers at the wall?"

"This isn't funny, Samantha," she whispered, suddenly clutching my arm. "We should call someone."

Obviously it wasn't funny. I was trying to calm myself down as much as Rebecca, since my heart felt like it was going to beat a hole through my chest, and not only at the thought of how long this would take me to get cleaned up. "I don't even know who you're supposed to call for something like this."

"The police, Samantha. You're supposed to call the police. You said you have the detective's card. Call him now," Rebecca said, pulling firmly at my arm as if to get out my phone herself.

"Rebecca, I don't think the police care about something like this. I know it's a big mess, but I don't think anything is even broken – not really. And look around, it doesn't seem like anything is missing." Although, in fairness, there was so much stuff it would be impossible to tell instantly if anything was gone.

But I pulled out my phone anyway, snapping a picture of the wall. I sent it to Arun in reply to his text, adding a caption: *Well this just happened. Otherwise good.* I debated which smiley face emoji was most appropriate before choosing the one I always went with, smiley face with sunglasses.

He called me almost immediately. I had to wrestle myself out of Rebecca's grip just to get the phone up to my ear.

"Leave it to an art student to come up with vaguely threatening art-related graffiti," were his first words.

"Yeah, absolutely the kind of clever joke I want to come home to on a Sunday evening."

There was definitely some kind of "Sunday scaries" joke in here somewhere, but unfortunately the deafening sound of my own heartbeat was still making it hard to think.

"Do you want me to come over and help clean it up? I'm sure we have some paint lying around in the basement – we could get that wall redone pretty quickly."

"Yes, yeah, I mean. Thank you, yes. That would be great." Smooth, Sam. Very smooth.

"No problem, I'll be over in about twenty."

Great, about twenty minutes to brush my hair and change, so I could pretend I hadn't been wearing a pink, paint-stained sweatsuit all day, and definitely owned and actually used a hairbrush, like a normal person.

"Who was that? That detective?" Rebecca was still standing in the middle of the room, starting to look slightly ridiculous dressed in her full winter getup of puffer jacket, beanie, and mittens.

"No, actually. It's Arun, Stephanie's brother? I think you guys have met once or twice at their store. He's been helping me a bit with looking into Catherine's death." I rushed on, trying to head off Rebecca's glared warning at the pass. "He's a journalist! So, you know. He knows how to investigate things. Responsibly, of course. He's trained for this, Rebecca."

"Fine. I'm just glad you called someone."

Called a man, we both thought but didn't say. I know I should hate the feeling of wanting to be rescued, but sometimes, like when someone has broken into your house, trashed your bedroom, and left vaguely threatening graffiti on the wall, it just feels good to have someone around who's a lot closer to six feet tall than you are.

"We should check out the rest of the place," said Rebecca. "Make sure nothing else is wrecked or missing."

We spent half of my valuable hair-brushing minutes turning on every light in the apartment, and it quickly became clear that only my room had been messed with.

Arun, true to his word, showed up in exactly twenty minutes, lugging two cans of paint, a paint tray, and two rollers up the stairs.

He let out a low whistle as I ushered him into my room. "I didn't know you were this messy, Sam."

"Nice to know you think this is a good time to tease me," I said.

Arun grinned but his expression quickly became serious as he turned towards the wall.

"What do you think this means?" he asked. "What is it you really can't do without pain?"

I closed the door to my room to keep Rebecca from overhearing us, even though she had already removed herself to take, as she said, a restorative bath, which we both knew was code for hiding in the bathroom with a glass of wine while watching calming animal videos on Instagram.

"I mean, this is obviously about Catherine. I spend all week talking to people about her death, asking all these questions, and now this? I don't see how it could be anything else."

"Agreed," he said, moving forward and running a hand across the first letter, "Y." He held up a newly brick red finger. "It's still pretty wet. How long were you guys out just now?"

"Not too long. I went over to school around noon and worked there all afternoon before meeting Rebecca for dinner, but she was home all day. So the apartment was only empty from about six to maybe half an hour ago, so about eight pm."

"So someone came in, did all of this, and got out again within the last two hours. Do you think a lot of people know where you live? Or does anyone else have keys?"

We didn't throw a lot of parties, but enough that the list of people who knew where we lived was long, and I said as much. "But only Benny and a friend of Mel's have spare keys. Mel's friend hardly knows me, and Benny said he was working at school, or else he would have been with us at dinner."

Arun nodded, still studying the graffiti. "So the real question is, who did you threaten into reacting like this? What was the one question you asked that put someone over the edge?"

Great, thanks, Arun. Definitely not the most terrifying way to phrase that. Although as he spoke, I knew who the first suspect should be. I explained about Friday evening, and my search through Ricky and Dan's rooms.

"Honestly, I can't really see Ricky doing this," I said. "If she felt threatened by me, she would probably do something quieter and more effective, like talk to the police or the administration about me. Or even just start some kind of nasty rumor. But the other roommate, Dan. He may have a more personal reason for doing something like this." I hated the questioning upswing I put on that sentence, like I was the one who should be embarrassed about what had happened. I took a breath and continued. "I was in the middle of going through his room, which, by the way, was about as messy as this is now," I gestured to my things strewn around. "And he came in while I was there, and he kind of … got the wrong idea about what I was doing in his room." I paused, willing Arun to put the pieces together, but he just continued to look at me thoughtfully. "Well, I eventually had to make it clear that I wasn't there to hook up. And he didn't take it especially well. In fact, I didn't know he really had a temper like that until I saw how he reacted to my turning him down."

Arun considered this. "That would make sense. You didn't just tell him you had a boyfriend or something?"

"Uh, no. I guess that would have made sense, but. No, I'm not seeing anyone right now."

"Cool, cool. Right," Arun said, turning fully back to the wall now.

Wait, what? Was he really just trying to find out if I had a boyfriend? I tamped down on my inner thirteen-year-old, who was currently screaming inside my head.

"Let's get a few more pictures of all this, and then we should probably get started cleaning up." Arun did a three-sixty turn in the center of the room, snapping a panoramic view of the mess. He paused, phone still in hand. "You know, if you wanted, I could do a little more digging at work tomorrow. Maybe look up Dan and whomever else you've talked to, see if anyone has police records or anything else out there that might be suspicious."

"Of course that would be great. I'll text you a list of names."

Of course it would be great for me to have another excuse for calling him.

Rebecca appeared in the doorway, wrapped in a huge bathrobe, glass of wine still in hand. She surveyed the room grimly, smiling only to acknowledge Arun. "Do you guys need any help in here?"

"No, honey. You go lie down," I said, picking up a stray sweater from the floor by my feet and tossing it back into the open dresser. "See? We're basically done already. No problems here."

I pictured a smiley face emoji at the end of that sentence, of course with sunglasses.

Chapter Ten

A run left by midnight, not before making more than a few jokes about how I was so messy to begin with, you could barely tell the room had been tidied up. Unfortunately, the smell of fresh paint stayed much longer, becoming a nauseating alarm clock that woke me early the next morning. I had almost invited Arun to stay over last night but couldn't come up with a good enough reason why a sober adult man couldn't walk the six blocks back to his own apartment. Now, too nauseous to do much more than comb my hair with my fingers and try to pull on clothes I didn't wear yesterday, I was glad I hadn't.

The morning passed by uneventfully enough, my sculpture studio class a blur of student critiques, Agnes's voice a soothing hum in the background. It wasn't until I was walking through the lobby after class that I was jarred awake.

"Sam, hi, honey. How are you doing today?" Benny had suddenly appeared in front of me, his arms full of his now ever-present colorful flyers, with the new addition of a bullhorn. "Rebecca told me what happened last night. You must have been terrified."

He reached out to brush my hair out of my face, only lightly bumping me with the bullhorn in the process.

"Oh, yeah. It was pretty scary to come home to, but we at least got it all cleaned up."

"I know, I'm sorry I couldn't help, but I was tied up here all night." Benny continued his brushing and knocking. "Are you going to go to the police? You can't just let something like that happen without reporting it."

"No, I don't think so. I wouldn't have thought the police cared about something like that, someone just messing up my room. And besides, we cleaned it up already."

Looking over Benny's shoulder, I was aware that the lobby was slowly filling up with people, students trickling down staircases and out of classrooms, beginning to mill around in small groups. I guess my mental notes weren't foolproof, as I had completely forgotten that today was Benny's mental health event.

"Okay," Benny said slowly, as if saying each letter individually. "Just be very careful, okay? I couldn't stand it if anything happened to you."

I jolted back to attention at that. The break-in had been alarming, sure, but I hadn't really been thinking that it was only a prelude to a worse attack. Like one in which someone would actually try to harm me. Surely it was just a prank, Dan getting back at me for rejecting him?

"So?" Benny was waiting for an answer to a question I hadn't heard. "Are you coming to the rally now?"

"Oh, no, honey, I'm so sorry. I have to get to work in the library now."

I had never been so thankful to have a job as I was at that moment. Large groups of shouting people, especially if one of them has a bullhorn, has never been my thing. But it also occurred to me that now might be my best chance to try to find out if Dan had an alibi for last night. "I am really sorry, I know you've been working so hard on all this." I paused, trying to figure out how to get to the question I really wanted to ask. "Have you had any help on this?"

"Obviously Rebecca's been so supportive. And then I had to bring this whole stack of work home with me last night, petition forms and resource brochures and everything, and Ricky and Dan were so sweet." Benny shifted the stack of papers from one arm to another, as if to emphasize the weight of the project. "The three of us were up till midnight finishing everything up."

I agreed that this was indeed very sweet of them, gave Benny a peck on the cheek, and started to weave my way through the crowded lobby and over to the stairs that led up to the library. So, Dan was working late at home. But Benny never said when they started; at best, this was only half an alibi. He could still have had plenty of time to trash my room and then get back to help Benny fold brochures.

I paused on the staircase, turning back towards the lobby at the shrill sound of Benny's bullhorn crackling on. He was now perched on a small table, thanking everyone for their presence and support, giving directions to organize the crowd into a neater formation. I could see Rebecca standing just behind him, gazing up like a proud mother hen. Even Mel had put in an appearance, though she seemed more absorbed in her phone than in what Benny was saying.

"And I really have to thank our faculty supporters. We would never have had the confidence to approach the administration – no matter how absolutely vital and important these issues are – without their encouragement." Benny paused for a light smattering of applause. "A big thanks especially to Professor Thompson, for fielding and replying to my many, many emails about the administration and their responsibilities." Benny held out a hand, picking Thompson out in the crowd and pausing for a slightly louder smattering of applause.

Thompson stood off to one side, waving away the applause with the faux modest aplomb of a starlet winning an award. Huh. I had no idea that he and Benny were close, or at least close enough to have lengthy email conversations about school issues. I knew Benny had been involved in one or two other campaigns in the past, so perhaps it wasn't too unusual that their paths had crossed. I guess I just hadn't known that Benny was so passionate about paper straws being used in the cafe.

As I continued up the stairs and got settled in at the library circulation desk, I had to wonder: what if this was just a distraction? What if Thompson was down in the lobby right now, making a big show of how committed he was to the students and their well-being, only to distract from the fact that he had recently helped one of those students to her untimely end? Was this a big campaign or a little red herring? I accepted a stack of books being returned by a student and looked down at the first book on its way back to the shelf: *Medieval Animal Tapestries*. Okay, so the images of marauding lions and dragons would probably not help me to think clearly and calmly.

I got up and grabbed the cart full of books to be reshelved, glancing briefly at the first title before pushing the cart towards the section full of artist monographs. My Clue board was still as full as the cart. Perhaps it was just the library setting, but as I weaved in and out of the stacks, reshelving books on stained glass, post-modern furniture, and printmaking, I realized that what I really needed was some good old cross-referencing. I had people with strong motives for wanting to hurt Catherine. And I thought I had at least a few people with access to the means to do so. So now, I just needed to see who had both. I kicked myself for not realizing this sooner. And here I called myself an Agatha Christie fan.

Once the cart was emptied, I settled back at the desk, opening my phone to the Notes app and adding in a small, two column table. On one side, everyone with a motive: Dan, Ricky, Thompson, Chris. Michael, if in fact he did want to get back together with Catherine and had been rebuffed. The second column for people with the means and ability to tamper with her medications was a bit trickier. It might have been an overactive imagination, but I could see how anyone might be able to finagle access to Catherine's meds. Thompson, during a studio visit. Michael, while they were hanging out. If Catherine had left her bag in the studio unattended, anyone could have walked right in. Diabetes supplies weren't exactly in hot demand among the recreational drug crowds here, so I didn't think that Catherine would have reason to be particularly careful about where she left her bag.

In the background, I could hear the shouts and cheers of the rally still going on. It sounded like Benny was reading from a list, in between the cracks and squeals of the bullhorn. Maybe it was just this feeling of distraction, but I was starting to feel a bit of doubt creep back into my thoughts. If I was really being honest, I would have to admit that it seemed unlikely that Thompson would be able to gain access to Catherine's things. If she had gone to the bathroom or something while they were working together, she would have taken her purse. And if I was letting in that doubt, I would also have to admit that I wasn't even sure if Thompson knew that she was diabetic in the first place. It was even less likely that he knew where I lived, or thought I was a big enough threat to warrant breaking into my house and painting a few somewhat threatening words on the wall. I sighed, clicking my phone shut. I wanted Thompson to be guilty, because, let's face it, he seemed like a pretty bad guy all around. But Catherine wouldn't be best served by my chasing down the first creep who seemed even remotely like a suspect. No, I would have to focus on the facts. Like the fact that if I was looking for a pretty bad guy who actually had easy access to her meds and had recently demonstrated how angry he got when rejected by a girl, I wouldn't have to look any farther than Dan.

I shook my head, trying to clear out this messy web of names and motives. For the next hour, I focused on my work, becoming absorbed in the task of helping a student find books for a research paper on historical paper-making methods. It was as I was finishing up a demo for him on how to use our article databases that Ricky waltzed in through the library doors.

She waved at me, shaking a couple of books in my direction before placing them (and her arms) on the circulation desk. "Just returning these, Sam. How's it going?"

"Good, it's going pretty good," I said, trying to demonstrate the lower volume level she should have been speaking in. "How're you guys?"

Guys, plural, because she'd waltzed in with Michael. I made a mental note (and then an additional note to try to actually remember this one) to ask Mel what was going on with them. I definitely remembered them dancing together at Ricky's party, and if anyone would know if anything else had happened, it would be Mel.

"Pretty good, still the usual." Ricky grinned, leaning off the desk enough to lace her arm through Michael's.

Well, I guess that answered that. More or less. I was never very good at guessing other people's relationship status, and frankly didn't much care about anyone's but Arun's.

"Still recovering from the weekend!"

"Of course, happy birthday again," I said.

Michael, at least, had the grace to look a bit sheepish throughout this exchange, failing to meet my eyes. I know people grieve at their own pace and I shouldn't be one to judge, but less than a week ago he was telling me how upset he was over Catherine, that they might have been on their way to getting back together, and now here he was, letting Ricky lean herself against him like he was an obliging telephone poll.

"Well, I have to be getting back to it," I said, gesturing to the two books currently waiting to be reshelved, as if this were an insurmountable workload.

"Yep, us too, always more to do in the studio!" Ricky gave her little wave again, Michael offering a curt nod, as the pair started to make their way back out.

I came around the desk, waiting for Michael to get ahead a few steps before calling out (quietly) to Ricky.

"Actually, Ricky, do you have a sec? There was something I wanted to ask you. For class."

Ricky turned, still smiling at me as if she had all the time in the world to help a poor idiot with class work. I pulled my phone out as she came closer, clicking open to the photos I had taken in her room that weekend. I didn't say anything, wanting to see what her initial response would be, and just held the phone out so she could clearly see the screen. I even considered taking out the insulin vial protector I had found in

Dan's things. It might not have been in Ricky's room, but she would have had every opportunity to plant it on Dan.

Ricky's smile faded as she took in the image of the three snapshots of Michael clearly sitting on her bedroom floor. Her face hardened and you could clearly see the change coming over her features, as she seemed to choose not to be embarrassed.

"Why are you showing this to me, Samantha?" she hissed. "And how did you get these photos?"

I put the phone away before she could try to take it. "Just curious if Michael knows that you have photos of him hidden under your dresser. Not sure if you showed him these, Friday night? Or told him what you had done with them?"

Ricky did have the grace to try to look confused at least. "What I did with them? Nothing. I have photos of everyone. We were working on a yearbook, casually."

Sure.

"And this yearbook was going to come with a bundle of sage?"

Ricky's resolve visibly hardened. "Whatever, Samantha. I've done nothing wrong. And even if I did, I don't have to answer to you."

She spun hard on the heel of her boot and stormed out of the library, pushing violently against the heavy doors.

As the doors opened, a cheer traveled up from the lobby. Maybe I had to abandon my pretty bad guy theories all together. Because, judging from the look on Ricky's face and that proprietorial arm-grabbing of Michael, no one had benefited as much, as clearly, from Catherine's death as Ricky had.

At the pinging of a cell phone, I looked out at the room of assorted students studying, ready to shoot out a withering librarian look before realizing the phone was my own. I felt my stomach drop at the sight of a text from Arun. Followed, of course, by the stern internal voice that kept my inner teen in check. It was just business with Arun, after all: *You free tonight? I had some time today to look up the names you sent. Thought it'd be easier to go over in person.* Though, no matter how sternly I tried to talk to myself, I couldn't stifle the flutter of excitement.

Unfortunately, my "I have to work" excuse didn't hold up the following day. Which is how I found myself in the dean's office after the morning session of "Mineral, Mud, Clay," seated next to Benny in the kind of half-cushioned armchair you only ever see in middle schools and offices of middle managers. Across from us, in a far more comfortable, definitely three-figure desk chair, was Dean Winters, currently steepling his fingers as if deep in thought over the list Benny was running down, detailing the various demands that had been decided on at yesterday's event. I heard Benny on point number four, twenty-four/seven access to the counseling department, and tried hard to pay attention to point number five. But all I could muster was nodding along while my mind wandered to my conversation with Arun the night before.

I had met him at the Phans' store, where he was supposed to cover for Stephanie, who was going out on a blind date. After we both sat through her refresher on using the cash register, we got down to business. Luckily, it was a slow night, and we were only interrupted a couple times, mostly by kids looking for snacks.

"So I looked up all the names you sent," Arun had said, ticking them off on his fingers. "Suspects one through three, no police or court records, nothing of any interest."

Okay, so we had leapt right to calling them suspects. In my

own head, I was still trying to picture them as Clue playing cards, as if this softened the reality that we were investigating a murder. In any event, this meant that Ricky, Chris, and Dan had never done anything to get themselves arrested.

"But suspects four and five, Michael Drexler and James Thompson? They both had a couple of items in the database." He had brought his laptop down to the store and turned it around now so I could see from where I was standing, across the counter from him. "Michael has one arrest on his record, from two years ago for pot possession. He had just a little over the legal limit, so they gave him a few hours of community service and left it at that. So, no big deal." Arun paused to make sure I was in agreement.

I nodded. I couldn't see drugs coming into this at all. Catherine was never judgmental about things like that, so I don't think she even would have cared, if she had known.

"But now, here're the records for your professor, James Thompson." Arun scrolled to the next page, which showed some kind of legal document with a large, Massachusetts state government letterhead. "First, we have a record for his divorce from ten years ago. This is just a copy of his divorce certificate, no breaking news there. But then I also found this in the police records." Arun again scrolled down, to a form with handwritten notes, some kind of document I had never seen before. "Five years after the divorce, police were called out to a domestic disturbance at the house where his ex-wife was living. From the report, it sounds like she called the cops during an argument that became heated. A few plates and a vase broken, things like that." Arun paused, letting me catch up and skim through the notes. So far, it was exactly as he said. "When the police got there, it seems like there might have been a bit more going on.

I mean, they don't spell it out, but reading between the lines, it sounds like she looked as if she had been attacked recently."

I swallowed rising bile as I kept reading. Arun was right: the police never came out and said explicitly that the woman had been hit, but they note that she "appeared distraught," with signs of "possible contusions" on her arms. Or, as Arun was saying: she was distraught because her ex-husband had just attacked her.

"Do they ever say what the argument was about?" I asked.

Arun shook his head. "No, and because she didn't press charges, nothing goes any further than this police report. And most of the divorce records aren't public, although I put in a request so that we can see if there's any hint of whether this was a one-time thing, or something that had been going on while they were married and might have been the reason they split up." We were interrupted at that point by a mom being led into the store by her two young boys, who were gleefully allowed to pick out one snack each, while the whole time they were singing some song about cheeseburgers.

Arun had put the laptop away when they came in, and it seemed like this was the signal our conversation was ending. I stalled. "So basically, what we found is one probably meaningless arrest for drugs, and that one person turns out to be violent towards women, which makes sense since we already thought he was a jerk, to say the least."

I was pretending to mull this over while really I worried that my "we" was overstepping, but Arun didn't seem to notice.

"Agreed, it seems like this is the only person with any sign of past, potentially similar behavior."

"Plus, it shows that he can hold a grudge for some time. If Thompson attacked his ex-wife five years after their divorce –

and we're assuming it was the first time he'd done something like that – then it's possible that he had been stewing over whatever the trigger was for all those years."

Which meant, unfortunately, that if he had had a reason to attack Catherine, it might not even be for something that she had done recently. I would somehow have to comb back through two years of anecdotes and half-remembered rumors, to see if there was even a hint of something going wrong with them before.

"Sam, wouldn't you agree?" I snapped back to attention at the sound of Benny's voice. I got the distinct impression that his voice was raised because this wasn't the first time he'd had to issue the question.

"Yes, absolutely," I said quickly. "It's extremely important."

"It's extremely important that our next meeting be on March 15th, not March 18th?" Dean Winters raised his eyebrows at me.

"Well, yes. Of course," I stammered, blushing. "It's important that we work through this quickly. Especially once Catherine's memorial show is open, we should make it clear that we're working on more than just an exhibit for her." Good save, Sam.

Benny beamed, apparently satisfied with this response. He stood, gathering up the various outlines and petition forms that had been strewn across the dean's desk, and thanked the dean for his time, heading out while I sheepishly hurried after him.

"I think that went well," Benny said once we were back out in the hall, striding out to the lobby. "Now we have to just wait and see what actually gets done. But at least we communicated well."

"Yeah, you did a great job. Really, you should be proud." All of a sudden, I became aware of a migraine pushing against the back of my eyes. I was almost running to keep up with him and stopped suddenly, putting a hand up to my head. "Look, Benny. I have to get out of here."

He looked back at me with almost cartoonish concern.

"Okay, Sam, honey. You go home and get some rest. I'll see you tomorrow for Catherine's show installation." Benny tried to go in for an awkward hug, but his arms were too full of papers.

We had reached the lobby and I started taking small sideways steps over to the front doors. "I'm just suddenly feeling really sick. A migraine. I'll see you later." I rushed over to the doors before he could say anything else, yanking open the heavy glass and gulping in lungfuls of the cold air. It hadn't been a lie. I was suddenly feeling sick, almost dizzy with disorientation. I guess that's what I got for spending the better part of an hour with my mind wandering, checked out from what was actually going on around me.

Unfortunately, it seemed like my punishment wasn't over yet. Barreling down the walkway, I careened headfirst into Dan, coming face to face with his teal puffer vest, worn over a ratty flannel button-down. It was nearly twenty degrees outside; the guy might as well have been wearing shorts.

I mumbled an apology and tried to sidestep him, but he shifted his weight to block me.

"No worries, Sam. I'm glad I ran into you." Oh joy. "I wanted to apologize for the other night."

This was unexpected. I looked up as he continued, but his face seemed genuinely serious.

"Yeah, I'm sorry for being a jerk on Friday. I was pretty drunk and was probably meaner than I should have been about the whole thing." He waved his cigarette-holding hand as if to demonstrate the triviality of "the whole thing."

I bit back a response about what level of meanness would have been more appropriate, struggling not to say something about him being "probably" meaner than I deserved.

I shoved my hands into my coat pockets and raised my shoulders up to my ears, tucking my chin down in my classic Boston winter stance, trying to make it clear that I was intent on going on my way. But as I slid my hands into the coat pockets, my fingers connected with something smooth and plastic, and I hesitated before trying to walk away again.

"It's all good, Dan. But I did have something I wanted to ask you." I pulled out the insulin vial protector I had found in his room, holding up the small bottle so we could both examine this pink plastic object. "Just curious why you had this shoved away in your laundry?"

"I have no idea what that is. Is it one of your miniatures?" His bafflement seemed genuine, though perhaps the look of confusion on his face veered too far into caricature.

I rolled my eyes, trying to convey that I wouldn't put up with him playing dumb.

"No, it's not mine. It was Catherine's." I waited for him to say something, but he continued to stand there looking confused. "It's an insulin vial protector. That Catherine would have kept with her diabetes medications? That whoever tampered with her meds might have taken?"

"What the hell are you saying? Are you accusing me of something?" The same hard look I had seen on the fire escape came into his eyes. "Look, Sam, I'm sorry about the other night. And I'm sorry about whatever grudge you're clearly holding against me, but I've done nothing wrong. I never took anything of Catherine's, and I wouldn't even know what medications someone takes for diabetes in the first place." He dropped his cigarette, crushing the butt under his heavy boot. "But unless you have some other ridiculous claim to make against me, I have to get to class now."

With that, he pushed past me and into the building, leaving me standing there dumbfounded. Whatever grudge I had? In the voice silently screaming in my head, I added about ten question marks to that sentence.

I walked down the cobblestone sidewalk, taking a left on autopilot. After nearly three years here, I had my routine down pat for when I had to get away from school, when I needed some time to sit and think. Probably no surprise here, but it involved an art museum.

Chapter Eleven

I kept my mind clear as I walked towards the nearest pedestrian bridge that crossed the Charles River, focusing on taking deep, even breaths of the icy air. The pedestrian bridge I used most was only a few blocks away, and I paused in the middle of it like I always did. In one direction, the river pointed in towards Boston, now a landscape of boats wrapped up in swaths of shiny white vinyl, stacked for the winter. In the other direction, it was all trees and the river winding out towards Cambridge, and eventually the suburb of Watertown. I always took a minute to pause here, to notice the texture and the color of the water. I could cross this bridge every day and still always see the water differently. Today, when the sun was mostly covered by a dense blanket of gray, the water appeared almost black, with the surface eerily still.

Once across the bridge, I continued down the path that ran alongside the Charles, dodging the occasional biker and group of moms with strollers. In the summer, I would often jog along this path, pausing to rest on one of the benches, but now I hurried on against the cold, keeping my head down and seeing the river only out of the corner of my eye. I focused on the path, the gravel and dirt pockmarked with icy puddles. It was not lost on me that the metaphorical path I had been on this past week was similarly marked with icy obstacles. Some undoubtedly of my own making, from an active imagination saturated with one too many whodunits.

After about a mile along the river path, I veered right, crossing the street towards Harvard. Weaving through the groups of tourists and students in Harvard Square, I made my way through the Yard, towards the art museum, not slowing down until I was walking up the stone steps at the entrance. Only then, in the airy warm atrium at the entrance, did I stop, unwinding my scarf and taking a deep breath. Despite the echoey, open space, it was quiet and peaceful here.

I strolled through the current exhibitions, taking in a show of Renaissance women painters and a group of prints about historic Harvard architecture. I stopped at a few pieces along the way: a Renaissance view of Judith holding the head of Holofernes (a gory classic); a Greek coin with a satyr on it (I made a quick sketch for my urns); a painting of two women by a local artist working in the early twentieth century. The painting, *The Family*, showed two women standing with their backs to the painter, one sister looking over her shoulder towards him. The second sister has one arm around the first, her other hand held behind her back, with her fingers in some kind of enigmatic gesture. The painting is dark, all umber and verdigris fabrics against the stark brightness of the sisters' pale skin. I had probably passed by this painting a dozen times before, giving it little notice, but something about it seemed oddly compelling today. All throughout the museum, but especially in front of these two women, I had felt like an antenna, receiving some staticky, far-off signal through the hairs on the back of my neck, hairs that had been standing on edge since I got here. I shifted on my feet. Maybe I was just getting lightheaded from standing for too long.

I had a particular route that I always traveled through in this museum, starting on the ground floor and working my way up, always ending on the third floor. The atrium was open for the whole height of the building, so from the walkway here you could look down to the marble floors three flights below, or up to the fourth-floor research laboratories. The museum was famous for its collection of different kinds of pigments, showcased in cases upon cases and thousands upon thousands of bottles, in every shade imaginable, from ochre pigments that could basically be dug out of the ground and used without any processing, to newly minted colors made with complex formulas in company laboratories. I loved the possibilities these bottles contained, from natural pigments that were a perfect pine tree green, to the deepest black you could imagine, a synthetic pigment capable of creating visual black holes.

I leaned against the railing and looked up, taking in the now-familiar array of midnight blues, carmines, and umbers. It was only once I was here, the exact spot near the staircase that I always came to last, that I finally let myself think about Catherine. Calmed now from my walk and three floors of art, I could let myself admit the doubt that had been growing all day. Sure, I had been buoyed by my conversation with Arun the previous night, which did seem to cement the possibility that Professor Thompson was someone capable of harming a woman like Catherine. But lying in bed later that night, I'd had a sudden, almost panicked thought (and we all know the ideas you have right before falling asleep are your best ideas). It occurred to me that I could have been looking at this the wrong way all along. I had been considering all of these motives about

Catherine, about things she might have done (threatened to expose Thompson) or not done (rejected Dan). But what if the truth was something much more personal? About who Catherine was, not something she did.

Sorry, I don't actually have an immediate answer to that, just thought it would be a nice stopping point. Give the question more weight and all that. But I was not going to find the answer by staring into bottles of powdery pigment, as stunning as this array of colors might be. And that was okay: I just needed to admit to myself that I might have been going in the wrong direction.

No matter how many times you walk outside from inside during a Boston winter, the cold air is always shocking. I pulled my hat down as far as it would go over my hair, zipping my coat all the way up for my walk back to our apartment. Although it was only four pm, the sky was already darkening, with the ominous pattern of smooth, heavy clouds that could only spell snow.

As if on cue, my phone rang: Mom. Before I could even get a "hello" out, she was asking me about the weather.

"Samantha, are you sure you're well stocked? I was just looking at the weather and it seems like you guys could be getting a big storm tomorrow."

"Yes, Mom. All stocked," I replied, before promising her that I would stop for even more groceries on my way home, right now, even though the storm wouldn't start until overnight tomorrow.

"Okay, and hand warmers? What about gloves?"

Many more promises were made as to the contents of my closet and what I was currently wearing.

"Good, let me know how it goes." She paused, halting the preparedness questions momentarily, her voice softening. "And how is everything else, Sammy? How are you?"

"Actually, pretty good," I said, and realized I was really not lying.

I felt lighter from my afternoon away from school, my pondering while gazing at paintings. I caught her up on my school work, Rebecca, hanging Catherine's show tomorrow, and the parts of my investigation that felt Mom-worthy, glossing over the break-in and anything that might lead her to question me about Arun. We were still happily chatting away as I crossed back into Boston, the sun setting and the water a glistening black ribbon.

Chapter Twelve

By ten am the next morning, Rebecca, Benny, and I had managed to arrange a set of Catherine's paintings in a more or less neat row around the edge of the school gallery. The gallery had been a newer addition and something of an afterthought in the old building, shoved onto a corridor in the first floor, converted from a couple of old classrooms that had been knocked together. Windows ran along one side of the room, on a wall of white-washed brick. Great in theory, or in an architectural design magazine, but terrible when it came time to try to hang any kind of artwork on the brick, inevitably backlit and invisible against the windows.

The three of us stood back now, appraising the line-up we had just more or less amicably decided on. Whoever said that organizing artists is like herding cats had it absolutely right: it was something of a miracle that not only had we managed to pick out a selection of paintings together, but we'd even gotten them down to the gallery on the scheduled day. Even with the ever-responsible Rebecca involved, this had not been a guaranteed success. After all, she was balanced by Benny's inevitably pie-in-sky attitude, with him always wanting to do more than was reasonable, and my own carefully designed stance, of being present and helpful without ever taking on any real management responsibility. Now we were just waiting on help from the gallery staff to start hanging the work. I knew help would come in the form of a work study student and had my fingers crossed that it wouldn't turn out to be a particular teal-vest-wearing, massive-pile-of-laundry-having male student.

But, of course, luck wasn't on my side that day. Dan walked into the gallery now, carrying a four-foot level and pushing a utility cart full of assorted drills, fasteners, and wires.

"Morning, everyone," he said, nodding at Benny and Rebecca.

Apparently I was not a part of "everyone" and would be receiving the silent treatment today in response to my remarks about the insulin vial yesterday afternoon. That was honestly fine with me, as long as Benny and Rebecca didn't notice or assume it was for some other reason, especially for anything even remotely related to a failed hook-up.

I was content to hang back as Benny and Dan proceeded to mark off a spot for each painting, such that each would hang centered on fifty-six inches high, a gallery standard. I might have loved miniatures, but maintaining rigid ratios of 1:12 was never my thing; I was more than happy to leave the precise measuring to someone else. Rebecca walked along the wall with them, holding up each painting as necessary.

"Sam, how's this looking?" she called out now, holding the first painting in the line.

Catherine had finished this one earlier in the year, and it was a bit reminiscent of a Lucian Freud. It showed her and her mother as two figures entwined in an almost spherical ball, set against a rusty gray backdrop and overlaid with washes of ochre and orange, so that the whole scene had an autumnal glow to it. Against the clean white wall, it was a beautiful contrast. I gave Rebecca a big thumbs-up.

The three of them quickly developed a steady rhythm of measure, mark, and hang, working their way methodically down the wall over the next couple of hours. Everything was going so smoothly, and Benny even set up his phone to start playing music, some poppy '80s playlist that garnered a momentary, ever-so-slightly noticeable grimace from Rebecca. I guess, like me, she hadn't realized that hanging a memorial show for your dead friend could be such a cheery affair.

"R, did Sam tell you about the meeting on Monday?" Benny was asking Rebecca now, who shook her head.

"Only a bit, but it sounded like it went well?"

Benny nodded, momentarily silenced as he held a pencil in his mouth, his hands full with a drill and several screws.

"It definitely did!" he said, maneuvering the pencil to one side as if it were a cigarette. "I had an email from the dean this morning. They're still considering some of the requests, I guess working out the logistics. But, in the meantime, he said they're going to be able to start a scholarship in her name. It'll open next year."

I guess the meeting had gone even better than I'd realized and I kicked myself now for not paying better attention. Although, in my defense, I had been pretty preoccupied with solving Catherine's murder, so. It's not like I wasn't thinking about her.

"That's really wonderful to hear," Rebecca said, sounding sincerely on the verge of tears.

Benny put down his tools and went over to hug her, only letting go and turning around at the sound of someone else walking into the gallery.

"Thought you might need lunch!" Ricky chirped, swinging a white plastic bag of takeout towards us as she came into the gallery. She paused dramatically, putting a hand to her heart as she took in the paintings around us, about half of which were now on the wall. "Wow," she said, "Just wow. What an amazing collection of work." She shook her head, theatrically in awe of the show. I had to shut my eyes to keep from rolling them. "It's truly an amazing thing you guys have done here."

Rebecca and Benny thanked her, like normal people, while I stayed where I was, against the back wall where I had the distance to tell whether a painting was being hung crookedly. Ricky was unpacking the bag onto the utility cart, taking out sandwiches for her two roommates and Rebecca. I guess there had been some internal memo sent out that I wasn't to be considered a part of "everyone" today. Thanks, I guess I'll just go down to the cafe.

I tried to gauge Dan's reaction to all the talk of Catherine as he put down his tools and got up to grab lunch. But, like Ricky, he was studiously ignoring me, his face a meticulous blank. I sighed, edging around the group gathered around the cart and heading out the door. If I wasn't going to learn anything new by standing around watching four people eat sandwiches, I might as well get some lunch of my own.

Ricky had departed by the time I got back from my quick lunch break. Benny, Rebecca, and Dan had gotten back into the swing of hanging work and Rebecca quickly enlisted my help in the next step of affixing labels for each piece to the walls. The rest of the afternoon passed by smoothly, and we finally got all eighteen paintings up just as the sun was starting to set. Rebecca and I left Benny and Dan to tidy up in the gallery, and headed out together to walk back to our apartment.

Walking out of the gallery while still trying to get on all our various layers of coats and scarves, we both nearly collided with Professor Thompson.

"Hi, girls, excuse me," he said, neatly stepping around us and into the exhibit space. "Benny, hi there. Just wanted to see how you had got on today." He stood with his hands on hips, nodding as he assessed the placement of each painting, looking from one gray portrait to the next. "Great work, Benny. Really, it looks great here. Very professional." Thompson took a long stride over to Benny, giving him one of those manly handshake, shoulder pat combos.

Rebecca and I didn't wait to hear the rest of his praise and continued on our way, heading out of the building just as the first snowflakes were starting to fall. Again, I had to wonder: With his supportive, involved teacher act, was Thompson laying down a little red herring or a big glaring clue?

Chapter Thirteen

For once, my mother's worries about the weather were not overblown. By the time we woke up the next morning, classes were canceled for the day, with six inches of snow having fallen overnight and another five to eight forecast to come down by the end of the day. Bet you were thinking some big resolution would happen while we were all snowed in, right? Wrong. What is this, *Murder on the Orient Express*? We all just played Monopoly and broke our "no smoking inside" rule as soon as we could figure out how to disengage the smoke detector (though we left a chair in the hallway just in case someone had to quickly hit the button to turn it off again, you know, for safety). The three of us had put off homework, instead making pancakes and hot chocolate, taking a slippery walk around the block, and watching *Knives Out* for the umpteenth time. By this late in the day, all sequestered together, the three of us would usually start to get on one another's nerves, experiencing cabin fever in our own unique and generally incompatible ways. Really, we were normally great as roommates, hardly ever fighting. But on snow days, I was reminded that this was primarily because we were apart for work and school most of the time.

Like clockwork, at four pm, Rebecca had had a meltdown at the state of the kitchen post-pancakes, storming off to her room, no doubt to commiserate with Benny about what pigs we were. Mel, for her part, had started the day out in a bad mood, frustrated at being kept from the studio, but by late afternoon had mellowed, cheering up into a remarkably insufferable version of herself whom no one else was in the mood for. It was only after I had thoroughly checked every streaming app at our disposal and found absolutely nothing else worth watching, did I relent to Mel's entreaties, allowing her to entertain me with photos from the weekend's party.

She curled up next to me on the couch, leaning farther onto my legs than should have really been necessary, such that I had to fight off the urge to kick her away as she held her phone up to swipe through the various *Fresh Prince*, *Full House*, and *Boy Meets World* costumes on display at Ricky's party. So far, I had seen four senior girls dressed as two identical pairs of Mary-Kates and Ashleys, a dance floor full of couples and small groups barely identifiable in the dim lighting, and a close up of a smiling Benny, holding his drink with one hand and adjusting his Elaine wig with the other.

"Look, here's one of the whole group, all of us together!" Mel nearly squealed, showing me a dimly lit snapshot of Rebecca and me dancing together, Mel and Benny just behind us.

"The whole group," I said slowly. I could feel my voice rising in my chest. "All of us!"

Mel gave me a funny look as I shouted.

"Yes, Samantha, the four of us," she said, giving every syllable of my name its own beat. "You, me—"

"Wait, shut up. Hang on," I cut her off, gesturing for her to be quiet.

I knew I had just realized something important, something I was struggling to visualize, when my mind suddenly went back to Catherine's studio, like the kind of visual room you would use for a memory palace. No, not her studio. I turned my mind's eye towards the easel. It was the painting. This is what had bothered me from the start, in the photos the police had shown me of her studio. For two years, I had seen Catherine's paintings, at all stages from sketch to exhibit. And as far as I knew, she had only ever painted her and her mother, adding in different, blurred settings and backdrops, drawn from her own and stock family photos. When she'd died, she'd left a painting in progress out on her easel, a painting that was in the police photos and still there the morning I'd gone to look around. A painting with three figures. Catherine, her mother. And a male figure. What if Catherine had found out who her father was, and that's who was in the unfinished painting? What if she had found out, and it had somehow ended badly? I looked down, realizing my hands were bunched into fists in my lap. Mel was looking at me with raised eyebrows, clearly slightly pissed that I had told her to shut up.

I shook my head to clear it, as if thinking just happened on an Etch-a-sketch. "Sorry, sorry. Just remembered something I have to do." My whole body felt like a coiled spring, ready to burst into action. But as I looked towards the window, I knew I would have to relax: with nearly a foot of snow on the ground and more falling, no one was going anywhere soon. "It can wait. Keep showing me the photos," I said, struggling to turn my attention back to Mel's phone screen, as my body continued to tremble with this barely contained energy. Even if I could go out right now, what was I going to do? Run right to the police and tell them Catherine was trying out a new kind of painting, and that was the answer to everything? No. Before I could do anything else, I would have to go back to Catherine's studio. For all I knew, I could be remembering the painting completely wrong. Or maybe I was wrong about her never including a third figure before. I would have to check, to go back to where I'd started. Just as soon as I could get through the snow.

The next morning, I was out the door as quickly as I could manage, creeping down the creaky steps so as not to wake Rebecca and Mel. Knowing the bus would be a packed mess of slushy aisle and blasting heat, I chose to walk, going as quickly as I could through the snow. Where the sidewalks hadn't yet been shoveled, pedestrians formed a single file line that was agonizingly slow, and I almost fell into the knee-deep snow several times, trying to get around the crowds without stampeding.

Finally, I was at the art department building, hardly pausing to shake the snow off my boots before bounding up the stairs to Catherine's studio, holding onto the railing for dear life as my feet slipped around under me. The building was eerily quiet for a weekday, with most students still snowed in. I savored the peace for only a moment, the oily paint and damp clay smell instantly seeping bone-deep, before I made a beeline to Catherine's studio. It looked like Benny had already started the work of packing up her things, as I knew her aunt had asked him to. Thankfully, it seemed he'd focused on the desk so far, and the same painting still hung on the easel.

I gave it my full attention now, carefully studying the composition and figures. I wasn't wrong: there were indeed three figures. I could clearly recognize Catherine and her mother as the front two figures, images I knew from her other paintings. It was definitely the third figure in the background who was a new addition. I studied the face, trying to pick out any identifying details through the painterly blur. I thought there was something about the cheekbones, the set of the jaw that was vaguely familiar, but still too hard to place.

I opened one of the boxes Benny had already packed, met by a waft of turpentine. Here was a stack of earlier paintings, neatly tucked beside one another. I flipped through them, one by one, looking for any other painting with three figures. But again, it looked like I hadn't been wrong the night before: there were only ever two figures.

After a further ten minutes of failing to find the man in any other painting, I remembered what I should have all along: Catherine always painted from photographs. Which meant that there had to be a photo of this man somewhere, something that would show him far more clearly – and hopefully, more identifiably – than her palette of washed-out grays did. My eyes scanned the room and I started going back through the boxes I had already looked in, this time searching for anything resembling a snapshot, but with no luck. After a quick and similarly unsuccessful rummage through Catherine's supply cart, I shook out her sketchbook, even checking the back of the painting, hoping a scrap of paper or a Polaroid was taped onto it. As if this were a movie, and everything would just fall neatly into place now that I realized what I should have all along.

But if this was a painting of Catherine's father, and if Catherine's uncovering the truth about her parents had gone badly, then perhaps she would have intentionally tried to bury any photographic evidence. If I were Catherine and I wanted to hide something, I would try to find a hiding spot in a random object that wasn't obviously associated with me. I flashed back to an interview I had seen with the woman whose job it was to make disguises for CIA agents (a dream job if there ever was one), required viewing for a "Sculpture in the Movies" class I had taken the previous semester. She'd talked about using empty bricks and dead, stuffed rats for agents to do dead drops. My eyes fell on the stack of books on Catherine's desk, the legal title still on top. So what was the equivalent of a dead rat to a group of art students? A random book about the legal system from the law library on the other side of campus. A book exactly like the ones Catherine had checked out just before her death.

In my rush to get to the library and print out the rest of Catherine's check-out history, I knocked over the same painting in Benny's cubicle that I had messed up before. I righted it again, and again found my hand covered in the still tacky oil paint. In the back of my brain, a faint alarm bell was starting to ring. I chalked this up to the urgency of finding the photo, and bounded off to the library, nearly slipping in my still snowy boots.

Clutching the paper printout from the library in my gloved hand, I was making my way across campus, again having to slog through the crowded sidewalks, worse now as we approached the height of rush hour and as the snow rapidly became a dirtier, sootier mess of slush and ice. The law library was housed in an imposing brick building about ten blocks from the art department, home to an equally imposing set of law students. The college liked to promote itself as interdisciplinary, with students encouraged to take classes across the departments before settling on a major, but with the campus spread across all these city blocks, we inevitably wound up sequestered away in our own departments, where all of us art students couldn't stink up the rest of the place with our paint fumes.

Which is why it took me a few minutes of jogging down various fluorescent-lit corridors before I could even find the law library. The heavy wooden doors at the entrance listed an opening time a bit after our library at the art department, so I paced up and down the hall outside for a few minutes, trying not to rush the student who eventually came to open up. Once inside, I paused to take a deep breath, allowing the familiar smells of books and old paper to calm me for a moment, though these smells were joined by the very unfamiliar smell coming off the deep brown leather couches, which trumped our measly armchairs.

I knew I would have to be methodical in my searching, and quickly got to work, ticking off each book on the list as I went down the stacks. For each title, I would pull the book off the shelf and give it a quick flip through, to see if I would get lucky and have a photo just fall out. When that failed (each time), I would go back through the book, carefully turning each page, checking under the flaps on either cover. By book number five, the library began to fill up with students, settling in at the couches and the long rows of tables, each student tucked behind the mini dividers separating the tables into individual desks. I was suddenly aware of how out of place I looked, with the hair I still hadn't had time to comb, and the long, bright magenta parka I was wearing, standing out from this sea of black and brown wool sweaters like a traffic flare.

Luckily, I had a feeling that book number six would have the winning ticket: *Questions of Claims*, a book Catherine had checked out and returned two weeks before she'd died. A quick google search of each book as I slogged my way over here revealed that the claims in question were in fact paternity-related; it was a book about the judicial process of paternity claims and the rights one was entitled to once paternity was legally determined. Now that I thought Catherine had found her father, this book's title had taken on a whole new relevance, and I kicked myself for not seeing this sooner.

I pulled this book off the shelf, settling down onto the floor with the dusty book on my knees, its literal weight taking on new meaning. I imagined Catherine carrying this back with her all across campus, staying up late in her studio reading it from cover to cover. After my quick flip through revealed nothing, I started slowly turning each of its four hundred pages, my panic starting to rise as each page revealed not even a stray bookmark. There were only two more books on my list. If the photo didn't turn up here, I would have to come up with a plan B, and fast.

I slid my hand into the pocket for the card that marked check-out dates and beneath the crinkly plastic of the dust cover, feeling for anything that might be hidden between the cover and the dust jacket. Under the cover on the back of the book, my fingers connected with the hard plastic edge of something small and I felt my pulse quicken, my stomach starting to climb towards my throat. I pulled out a small, dark plastic square: a film negative that still had its sprocket holes on the top and bottom edges. I held it up, but the dim lights in the stack weren't strong enough to see the image clearly. I looked around the library, making sure there was no one around who would recognize me. I made my way over to the windows along the side wall of the library, cursing the loud rustle of my coat; I didn't need to look more like a noticeable weirdo than I already did. I held the small negative against the glass, letting my eyes adjust to the watery February sunlight. It looked like a photo from a newspaper, and showed two people at some kind of gate, or possibly ribbon-cutting ceremony. I could see a typed caption beneath it, way too small to read on the negative. Catherine must have taken a photograph of a newspaper page. Which meant, I thought, there was some reason she couldn't just keep the original newspaper. Or maybe she had, and it had already been removed from her studio by the time I was able to look through her things. Which meant that what I was holding was Catherine's insurance.

I stood frozen at the window, my fingers icy from where they were pressing the negative against the cold glass. I only moved at the sight of a boy coming towards me, with the universal look of a librarian coming over to help, which indeed is what he said as he approached. I quickly slid the negative into my pocket and turned away from the window, assuring him I was fine as I hurried out of the library.

I couldn't get into the darkroom to enlarge and print the negative until that evening, having to wait for the afternoon classes to empty out. I didn't want to have to answer any questions about what I was doing or why, or have to talk my way into a busy photo class. Instead, I spent the time until then trying and failing to pay attention during the rest of my sculpture studio class, to which I shuffled in, shamefully late and embarrassingly out of breath from my snowy sprint back to the art department building, and then trying and failing to pay attention during my afternoon shift in the library, barely making passable conversation when Benny stopped by to see if I wanted to go to dinner with him that evening. I think I mumbled something about working in the darkroom and made a mental note to text him an apology later. All I could think about was the negative, its little hard edges poking through my pocket. All afternoon, I furtively held it up to various lights, trying and failing to make out the figures in the image.

Chapter Fourteen

Finally, by six pm, the darkroom had emptied of other students and I slid in through the revolving blackout door, designed not to let even the slightest trace of light into the room. I stopped in the doorway, waiting for my eyes to adjust to the darkness. This darkroom was about the size of a generous living room, with stations for a dozen students to print at once, at the photo enlargers ringing the room around a central table, which held a series of trays full of chemical solutions that each photograph would be dipped into, before finally being washed in the running water at the end of the table and hung to dry. I loved everything about the darkroom: its theatrical single red light bulb in the middle of the room, the smells of the developer baths, and the sound of the running water amid the photos hanging overhead.

As much as I loved this room, I had not been down here for some time and it took me a few minutes to get the enlarger set up and turned on. Finally, the machine whirred to life, a sudden bright white light in the gloom of the darkroom. I took the small negative out of my pocket and slid it into the holder at the top of the machine, turning the various knobs to focus the image it projected onto the white of the table. I had guessed right: it was a photo of a page from a newspaper and it did show a ribbon cutting, with two people standing proudly behind the ribbon, above a neatly typed caption.

I was turning the levers to try to enlarge the text, even though it would just confirm what I could already see, when I heard the door slowly revolving behind me. Why had I chosen an enlarger across the room, such that my back was to the door? I was getting ready to tell off some freshman about the ways of the darkroom when I heard a familiar voice.

"Hello, Samantha." Familiar as it was, I had never heard such hardness in Benny's voice before. "Printing anything interesting?"

I fumbled for the switch to turn off the enlarger, suddenly very aware that I was looking at something I shouldn't be. Behind me, I heard the lock being flipped for the door, meant to shut out intrusions while printing, but now shutting me in. My stomach dropped to my feet and I could feel every hair slowly stand on end.

"Catherine was your sister," I whispered.

"Half-sister," Benny said sharply. "Not my actual sister."

My mind raced, trying to catalog every potential weapon in the room. Nothing within reach seemed like it would be useful to me, unless I could get Benny out of my way by throwing a negative holder at him, a piece of plastic that weighed about an ounce. But at least, I reasoned, that meant Benny was similarly limited in his available means to attack me. Unless he'd brought his own weapon, which was likely since I was now pretty sure he had already killed one person. Actually, I was quickly becoming positive that he had already killed one person. Thanks for that comforting thought, Sam.

I turned around, pressing my back against the enlarger and

desk. While I was scrambling for a weapon, I could see Benny had been taking slow steps towards me. I inched sideways, aware that I had a long way to go to get around the room and to the door.

"Why didn't you want a sister?" I asked, my voice suddenly loud (if quavering) in the quiet room.

I could see the whole situation now with a kind of clarity that I sincerely hoped didn't indicate that I was currently having a near-death experience. Catherine and Benny had grown up in the same town, best friends since elementary school. Catherine's mother had wanted to protect her daughter, not wanting to ruin Catherine's friendship or embarrass either family with the truth. I wondered if Benny's father ever even knew.

I could almost hear Benny's sneer. "Please, Samantha. Don't be childish. This isn't about sisters, best friends forever, and all that nonsense. Grow up."

Another step sideways. I would have to keep Benny talking if I had any hope of getting to the door. "So explain it to me. How did you even know about Catherine? About her mother and your father?"

Even without reading the caption, the photograph told a pretty clear story: at some point before either child was born, the two of them had worked together, their relationship memorialized in this photo of the pair at a ribbon cutting their company was involved with. I had seen enough television to know that apparently half the time, proximity was all it took to start an affair.

"She went behind my back," Benny growled. "She found some stupid photograph and then, for Christmas, she got us both those ancestry genetic test kits."

My mind flashed back to those emails over the winter break, Catherine and Benny in party hats in his parents' attic, sorting through childhood belongings. His father must have saved the newspaper clipping, perhaps out of some sense of sentimentality that I might not have expected from him.

"She told me a few weeks ago that the genetics showed we were a match as siblings. As if it were the best news in the world." Benny's sneer was getting louder.

And unfortunately, he was also getting closer, edging around the table.

I slipped my hand into my coat pocket, careful to keep the light of my phone facing inwards, so Benny wouldn't see what I was doing. I sincerely hoped that all those hours in class spent texting without looking were about to pay off. I tapped out a quick message to Stephanie. Or at least, I hoped I did.

"But it wasn't such great news?" I asked while typing, wishing I could keep the stammer out of my voice.

"Samantha, be practical. Catherine being my sister meant Catherine thinking she was entitled to a portion of my inheritance. My inheritance." Even in the dim light, I could see Benny's hand clenched into a fist as he brought it down onto the table for emphasis. "How on earth am I supposed to be able to be an artist without the inheritance? I can't have a job. I can't be taken away from my art. That inheritance was for my entire career." He sounded angrier than I had ever heard him.

I felt my own anger rising. I had known this person for three years, thinking what a funny, sweet, fun person he was, when all along he was really a selfish monster. A selfish, spoiled monster at that, who couldn't possibly be expected to have to live like the rest of us, who subscribed to some outdated ideal that an artist was only an artist if they didn't have to do other paid work. I took a deep breath and another sideways step, trying to put more space between us. I would have to ignore this rage and keep him on my side if I was going to get out of this darkroom. I screamed to Stephanie in my head, willing her to hear me.

"Of course, Benny. I understand," I said, doing my best to placate him. "So what did you do?"

I sensed a small smile from him, even if I could barely make out his face through the darkness. "Catherine had diabetes. She made a mistake with her medications."

God, even without seeing him, I could hear enough of the smugness to be able to picture his face clearly.

"Come on, Benny. This is me. How did you do it? The police didn't even think she had been killed."

He paused, clearly debating how much to tell me. I didn't think it was a good sign that he obviously decided to tell me everything.

"All I had to do was use one of her spare needles to combine a few vials of insulin into one of those insulin injectors she used. And then, like the helpful friend I am, I gave it to her when she needed it." Of course.

All that time I had spent trying to get into Ricky's and Dan's rooms, all that sorting through dirty laundry for nothing. Knowing Benny's meticulousness, the extra syringe would have been wiped clean of his prints and put back in Catherine's things, as if she had innocently used it herself. She might have noticed the empty vial protector, but surely no one would go digging through every last piece of Dan's laundry to try to find it.

By now, Benny had come around the edge of the table and was only a few feet away from me. I still had no idea what, if any, weapon he had brought in with him and I didn't intend to find out just yet. I would have to do my best to keep him talking, doing quick mental math to work out how much longer it would take Stephanie to get down here. If I was lucky, it might only be another five to ten minutes. If I was unlucky or had texted the wrong person, then it seemed likely the question of what weapon Benny was hiding would soon be answered. I took a deep breath.

"The wet painting," I said, louder than I meant to.

I had knocked it over twice in Benny's studio, and kicked myself for not paying better attention to those alarm bells earlier. If Benny had been working on the painting in the weeks before Catherine's death, it would have been dry by now. But, if he had in fact been with Catherine in the studios that night, well, the painting would still be wet.

"Yes, Samantha, the wet painting," he said as if I were a child who had to have it all spelled out for her. "I wondered if you would catch that. But you didn't."

"But how come the police didn't know you'd been here that night?" I asked, genuinely confused. I knew our security was somewhat lax, but there was still CCTV.

"I told Catherine to go ahead without me, that I was going to head straight home from dinner. Then I pretended to change my mind, and came in through the back entrance off the alley to the Humanities building. There's a connection to our building down here in the basement."

I didn't think his smugness could get any louder. I could feel my anger rising again, supplanting my equally mounting panic.

"And what about the mental health campaign? And the memorial show? Why go to all that trouble?" I could feel my limbs starting to tremble as I realized that Benny had been creeping along, step by step, in sync with me this whole time, and was now only a couple feet away.

"Who are you going to suspect? Some poor, grieving student who went to such lengths to remember his dear friend? Or some jerk who has an insulin vial protector in his closet? Or any of the other idiots you tracked down on your ridiculous wild goose chase."

Benny was just a couple of steps away from me now. As if on cue, the lock at the door began to rattle, slowly at first and then more urgently. At the sound, we both leapt, me towards the door and Benny towards me. I had a brief, brilliant flash of the ending sequence from *Rear Window*, and closed my eyes, straining up to flip on the nearest enlarger, giving myself a split-second head start as Benny fumbled blindly in the sudden light.

"Samantha!" a voice called from the hallway.

Arun was shaking the door now, audibly arguing with someone I assumed was Stephanie. I tried to call back, my voice coming out as a strangled cry, as suddenly, Benny was on top of me. We stumbled together, lurching this way and that as he dragged me towards the center table and the chemical baths. I might have loved the darkroom, but I certainly did not intend to die in a pool of photo developer. I kept trying to call to Arun, but heard only footsteps thundering down the hall in response.

Benny gripped me around the chest, his arms under mine in a classic lifeguard's carry, ironic, as clearly his intent was not to save me from drowning. I tried hard to kick myself free, twisting in his arms, though as my face inched closer and closer to the deep tub of liquids, I had to gulp in breaths, telling myself I could hold my breath long enough for Arun to get through the door.

My face had just grazed the liquid on the table, as finally, there was the sound of the lock being turned, more voices in the hallway. And then there were hands on us, arms pulling Benny off of me, the lights being switched on.

A couple of hours later, I was sitting on the back of an ambulance, a silver heat blanket draped over the pink coat I was still wearing, though it was now speckled with yellow dots and dashes down the front from where the darkroom chemicals had splashed onto us. As soon as the police left my side, having convinced them I would survive from my rugby match in the darkroom, I called Stephanie over to the ambulance, using her phone to check my face, dismayed to find a similar pattern of yellow splashes from where I had nearly been dunked in the chemicals. My own phone would be evidence until further notice.

"Bet you're pretty impressed with my texting skills now, aren't you?" I beamed, thinking I was finally due some smugness of my own, having gotten her here in the heat of the moment without even looking once.

Arun came over to join us, as he'd finished up his statement with the younger police detective, who, even from here, I could see had the grace to look sheepish.

"No," Steph said simply. "You texted the word 'help' followed by a bunch of autocorrected nonsense. But since we had turned on Find My Friends when I went back on Tinder, I was able to track your phone."

I saw Arun's jaw clench at the mention of his younger sister's dating life. Adorably protective of family? Check.

"Oh. Well, are you at least impressed that I, you know.

Managed to solve a freaking murder?"

"No," Steph repeated herself. "You nearly got yourself killed."

"Hey, go easy on her," Arun cut in. "We were all just worried about you," he said to me, adjusting the silver blanket from where it was slipping.

I shot Steph a look, smug after all.

Chapter Fifteen

About three weeks later, I found myself sitting at our kitchen table, in awe of the scene playing out around me: Arun chopping vegetables and stirring simmering pots on the stove, Arun mixing me a drink, Arun carefully lowering noodles into a pot. The minute he'd texted me earlier, asking if I was up for dinner, cooked at my place, naturally, since I was still supposed to be "resting," I had bundled Rebecca neatly off to take a bath and made sure that Mel was working late. Arun and I had been talking since the whole being saved from Benny debacle, texting jokes and silly GIFs back and forth between moments where he'd genuinely tried to check in on me, and this would be our first solo dinner. The last thing I needed was a nosey roommate putting him off.

Now, I smiled as I watched him stir, lifting up the pan to give the vegetables sizzling away a good toss. He caught me staring, and smiled back.

"So, no jokes this time. How's everything going, really? Has it been okay, being back at school?"

After being nearly drowned in the darkroom, it was decided that I should take a few days' leave from school. Time to recuperate, the administration had said. Quietly and out of the media spotlight was the implication, which had shone down on the college since it was revealed that Catherine's death was no accident. What this really meant was five days spent pacing around the apartment like a perpetual snow day, alone all day to watch all of *Downton Abbey* for the sixth time, before Rebecca came home to fuss over me and cook endless pots of soup. Can't say I really hated it.

"It's been fine, actually. Kind of surprising, I guess. I feel like some memo went out while I was absent, telling everyone not to mob me with questions."

It was true, which probably made it extra shocking the day when Professor Thompson came barreling down the hallway towards me, barking my name out from fifty feet away. I honestly considered running, but when every other head in the hallway had already turned towards him, it was hard to pretend I was the only one who hadn't heard him. As it turned out, he didn't want to yell at me. Well, not exactly. Everything that man says is basically shouted. What he really wanted to know was whether I was officially investigating him, that day in his office. I stammered about for a while, not quite knowing the ethics of admitting to this or not, but he assumed the correct answer from my hesitation. He had given me an appraising look. "Okay, Samantha. I have to say, I think I admire that. Good on you for taking this all on. That spot is still open to work with me next year, if you're interested." With that, he had sauntered off down the hall, aware that he still had everyone's attention. You could almost see him debate whether to throw in a wink. I couldn't in a million years picture myself working with that creep, but it was good to know that this whole thing hadn't exactly ruined my reputation or anything like that.

But for now, none of that mattered. Next year would happen,

and eventually we would move on from this whole awful episode. For now, all that mattered was that I was in a warm kitchen, watching this man fuss over sizzling pots, cooking me dinner, while I sat here, drinking my dark and stormy.

About the Author

Sarah Vernon is an author and artist based in Massachusetts, where she writes the Triple-Decker Mystery Series. You can find out more at vernonmysteries.com.